IT HAPPENED IN ZIHUATANEJO

E. Thornton Goode, Jr.

IT HAPPENED IN ZIHUATANEJO

iUniverse books may be ordered through booksellers or by contacting:

iUniverse
1663 Liberty Drive
Bloomington, IN 47403
www.iuniverse.com
844-349-9409

ISBN: 978-1-6632-3916-7 (sc)
ISBN: 978-1-6632-3917-4 (e)

Print information available on the last page.

iUniverse rev. date: 04/27/2022

In Appreciation

Once again, my friend, Galen Berry, has been so very helpful in the proofreading and editing of this work. Several suggestions he made were incredible to improve and enhance the storyline. He was so helpful doing the same with some of my previous novels now in print. I hope he will continue with the ones up and coming. Thank you, Galen.

I also want to thank Katherine Otis for her assistance in the proofreading and editing. She pointed out several things that needed to be corrected. Thank you, Katherine.

I want to thank my wonderful partner of nineteen years, Phillip McDonald, for letting me use his picture to show the reader the appearance of the character of Jacob in the story. Interestingly enough, Phillip was a fireman during his lifetime just as Jacob is in the story. Phillip caught a cold in early May 1996. He didn't take care of it, saying it would go away. In a few days, it developed into rampant pneumonia. A week later on May 10, 1996, he was gone. He was 48 years old. He was a kind, caring and considerate man. I can still see him smiling in my mind.

I want to thank my third partner, Julian Green, for letting me use his picture. It will give the reader an image as to the appearance of the character of Armando de Santiago in the story. The only difference is the color of the eyes. Julian's were an amazing blue and Armando's are green.

Julian and I became great friends, starting in 2009. It turned into a relationship after my second partner, Dan Glass, passed away from a heart attack on May 20, 2014. Dan was 55 years old. Dan was a funny and incredible man. He is truly missed.

Julian went in for a simple operation on December 16, 2017. It was a success but Julian went into an anesthesia coma. He was removed from life support and passed away on Christmas Day. He was 59 years old. The world lost an incredible artist and a wonderful, caring man.

I miss all three of my partners very much. Someone once asked me if I had known what was going to happen, would I have done anything differently. There's a country song sung by Garth Brooks and these are some of the important words it expresses: 'For a moment, all the world was right. How could I have known, that you'd ever say goodbye? And now. I'm glad I didn't know the way it all would end, the way it all would go. Our lives are better left to chance. I could have missed the pain, but I'da had to miss the dance.' Although there was great emotional pain, I was very lucky to get to dance three times.

Galen

Phillip

Dan

Julian

Bio Information

If you don't know by now, I will mention it again. I retired, sold the house in Atlanta back in 2013 and moved to the SW coast of Mexico in November of 2014. Love it here. It's summer all the time. Dan was supposed to be here with me, but he passed away six months before we were to come here. It's a shame as he loved the ocean and it is 400 feet from the front door.

This is novel number seven to go to press. If you want to know my other works that are published and in print, go to the following websites and search my name: buybooksontheweb.com and iUniverse.com

Right now, my main goal is to get all thirteen novels I've presently written and maybe my collection of short stories published and in print before I drop dead. GRIN! Presently, it is 2022 and with this COVID Pandemic crisis going around right now, one never knows. I have gotten two vaccine shots so far. Here is a picture of me before I got my shots, trying to stay safe. You all stay well.

—ᗰᗯ—

Stop laughing. I know you are.

Prologue

How many times have you heard the expression, no one ever says life would be easy or fair? Trust me. They are correct. It's not easy. And it definitely isn't fair. It's a series of forks in the road and we have to choose the ones to take. Every choice introduces us to new experiences, challenges as well as people. Sometimes we may reminisce about what it would have been like if only we'd taken another road. But unfortunately, we can't go back and change the past. Wouldn't it be interesting if we could?

Another question. Do you believe in coincidence? Well, I have to tell you. The Fates work in mysterious ways. Events we get swept into or people we meet along the way can be life-altering. In this writer's life, many things have happened, convincing me we're not in those events just on happenstance. And the same is true for the people we meet. It was for a reason.

A perfect example is the time a friend wanted me to go bar hopping with him. I did much begging and protesting not to go but finally, reluctantly, gave in to him. If I'd not gone with him that night, I may not have met the person who became a most significant individual in my life and with whom I began a nineteen-year relationship. That, of course, is one extreme example compared with smaller ones that have happened.

There are always those circumstances we hear of like being in the right place at the right time or possibly the wrong place at the wrong time. Regardless, I think they're all happening for some reason. We may never know why. But occasionally, we are lucky and can put the puzzle pieces together enough to figure it out.

What about those we meet and share our thinking and philosophies? Here again, I once met someone who explained something to me that threw a door wide open as well as my eyes to a significant issue of concern to me, allowing me to move on with a new awareness and perspective. I owe a huge debt of gratitude to that person.

So, think about it. Be aware. Events, people we meet and conversations we get caught up into could be for a reason. We may never know who's listening or seeing how we handle an event. Our words and actions may change our lives as well as someone else's. And who knows? They even may possibly change history.

CHAPTER I

Andrew stood, looking out over the ocean at the setting sun. The waves caught the bright oranges and yellows in the sky. The sound of the crashing waves was soothing. But nothing could stop the pain.

The pain was like the one he experienced less than a year earlier. He could recall it so well. It was like having it all over again.

Andrew shook his head. Here, it's happening again, and so soon. It isn't fair to be struck by lightning twice. Again, he felt he was cursed. Cursed to find someone wonderful, kind and caring, only to have that person swept away. Maybe he should be happy with the time he did get to spend with both of them. And maybe hell would freeze over, too. Maybe there would be world peace in his lifetime. Yeah! Sure! Believe it!

He began to think about how it all started just after the first of February, the morning after the big storm.

CHAPTER II

Andrew got up from bed. It was very early in the morning and the sunlight was slowly beginning to show itself. It was Wednesday, the first of February, 2006. His month-long vacation had just begun a few days earlier when he flew down the previous Sunday. This would be the first visit after moving things in a year ago. All he had to do was kick back and chill out for a whole month. It was not going to be easy. He should be sharing the time with Jacob.

"Zihuatanejo. The first time we heard that word Jacob and I were watching the movie, 'The Shawshank Redemption'. We thought it was a fake place." Andrew shook his head and chuckled. "Little did we realize at the time we were going to retire here. This close to Zihuatanejo. Yeah. Can you believe it?"

The previous day he got on his cell phone, calling the business to let them know he'd arrived safely. He had confidence in them to take care of everything and not to call unless it was absolutely necessary. Kenny was the main man there and had total ability to get things done. Kenny reassured him not to worry and to have a relaxing vacation and not dwell too much on last May. But Kenny just knew that would not be happening.

The heavy storm the night before was so unusual as this was not the rainy season. Andrew checked around on the terrace to see if the winds had damaged anything. The power was out. "I guess I'll get the candles out and use them this evening. And no opening of the fridge or freezer."

And with no power, the water pump would not be working. He was glad they had always kept a few bottles of water under the sinks in the bathrooms, so they could brush their teeth.

"That was some storm last night. I see it's imperative I get an LP generator." He shook his head. "Strange for a storm like that to happen in February. Rainy season doesn't start till mid-June at the earliest." He paused a moment. "Climate change. Global warming. That could be it."

Seeing all was secure and in place, he decided to walk down to the beach. The waves sometimes brought things to shore that were interesting. During his walk down, he reflected on how this new adventure culminated.

He'd come to Zihuatanejo to get a lot near the ocean. There, he and Jacob would build their retirement house even though it was 2004 and retirement was over twenty years away. But Andrew and Jacob were frugal and liked to plan for the future.

In his catering business, things were usually light in February and could be handled by his staff. This gave him the chance to come down and look around. Unfortunately, Jacob had his shifts changed because of an emergency in the department and had to stay behind, so he told Andrew to come and check it out. They both liked the area around Zihuatanejo, having visited several times on vacation.

Every time they'd come down, they would rent a car and stay at the same place in Troncones located some twenty-five miles up the coast from Ixtapa and Zihuatanejo. The people were incredibly kind, hospitable and helpful, never minding their inability to speak the language except for token phrases, telling them not to worry about it. They would smile as they told them it was okay.

The local economy made it a 'no-brainer'. He knew they could live here very comfortably on very little. And on top of that, the beautiful Pacific Ocean and the incredible weather all year round were significant pluses. Jacob so loved the beach. He was thirty-seven and quite pleased they had a plan for the rest of their lives.

During the first few days of his visit, Andrew discovered some land about forty-five miles north of Zihuatanejo. It was on the beach and was absolutely amazing. It was secluded and the beach was beautiful. There was no way they could afford a lot on the beach but even one lot back would be just fine. He knew it would be significantly less expensive than oceanfront. He just had to hope no major structure got built in front of them.

The sound of the surf was so relaxing. He watched it crashing on the many rock formations, projecting from the surface just offshore as well as the ones spotted up and down the beach. He knew this was the place for them.

It was early in the month when he walked into the government offices in Zihuatanejo to inquire about purchasing property. Sitting down with an extremely helpful lady named Consuelo, he pointed to a stretch of beach on a map she had placed on her desk. "I'm pretty sure the land I'm interested in is located in this area but I'm not quite sure of the exact spot."

She explained that she was very familiar with the property along that beach. It was part of a very large parcel owned by one family. It had been in their possession for over a hundred years. Regarding the purchasing of a lot in that location would mean he'd first have to go speak with the legal representatives for the family. It was a law firm located in the city, not far from the bay of Zihuatanejo. She said she was not very hopeful as there had been many who'd asked about property there over the years and no one had been successful in getting a lot anywhere on the parcel. She smiled at Andrew and spoke softly. "But it does not hurt to try, Señor. Let me call them and see if they are in today."

Andrew left her office with the directions on how to get to the offices. When he arrived, he came to a high-walled compound with metal gates at the entrance. Consuelo was correct. It was not that far from the bay. The gates were wide open as if inviting him in. Parking the rental car, he walked into the main building. The sign out front had very large letters: La Firma de Abogados Vargas. His Spanish was not very good but he knew it meant: The Vargas Law Firm. Entering, he walked up to the reception desk and spoke to the young lady, indicating he'd come to inquire about getting a lot on a parcel of property overseen by her law firm. She smiled and asked if he'd like a cup of coffee while waiting. He thanked her for her kindness, said he was fine then went and sat down.

Shortly, she led him into one of the offices. Behind the desk was a stocky Hispanic man in his early fifties with a big smile on his face. His hand was outstretched to shake Andrew's. "Manuel. Manuel Vargas. How are you, Señor?"

"Andrew Stevenson. I'm fine. Gracias."

"Where are you from?"

"I live in Atlanta. Atlanta, Georgia. In the States."

"Interesting. Andrew Stevenson from Atlanta. Very good." He looked hard at Andrew. "Señor Andrew. Excuse me for a moment. I need to check something." He left the room but returned after about fifteen minutes. He sat down and just stared at Andrew for a few seconds. "Interesting. Very interesting. Hmmm. So. From Consuelo's phone call, I see you are interested in getting a lot here in our country. She gave me your name and told me the area you are considering. I pulled out the land map." He looked very closely at Andrew. "Interesting. Very interesting." He paused for a moment, then pointed to the large paper on his desk. "Señor Andrew. This is the map of that whole area on the coast. The parcel owned by our client is outlined in red. As you can see, it is quite large. Is that the area where you seem to be interested? Can you show me about where you were considering?"

Andrew looked at the map but was not quite sure where it was he'd seen the place he wanted. "Yes. That is the area along the beach. But, geez. I'm not quite sure as to the exact location of the spot I am interested in."

"Just a second." Manuel went to his computer and pulled up a Google Earth satellite view of the area.

As it zoomed in on the global detail, Andrew could see the rock formations in the ocean and the little cove area on the beach very clearly. "That's it! Right there!" He pointed at the screen. "It's so beautiful there." He looked at Manuel and smiled. "I recognize the little cove. It would be a great place to put a small boat in the water."

"Yes. It is a very beautiful area. I believe it is one reason the family obtained the parcel so many years ago. Yes. Here is that spot on the map. Here." He pointed to the section of the drawing showing the little cove.

"Yes. That's it." Andrew pointed to the land near the cove. "This would be where I'd like to purchase a lot. Consuelo said it had been in the same family for over a hundred years." He bent his head down and spoke softer. "She also said no one had ever been successful in obtaining a lot there." He looked up at Manuel.

Manuel looked at Andrew, shook his head and smiled. "Very interesting. But maybe. Just maybe, it is time. Please. Take this pencil and mark the land map. Show me an approximate location where you would consider."

Andrew was stunned. Were they actually considering letting him have a lot? "Señor Vargas. I know I couldn't afford to buy a lot on the beach, so…"

"Señor Andrew. Do not think about cost right now. Let us say you have all the money in the world." He looked at Andrew and chuckled. "Where would you like to buy?"

Andrew couldn't believe his ears but obliged anyway. What could it hurt? All they could do was say… 'NO'. He took the pencil and drew a conservative lot right on the beachfront near the little cove. He knew it was probably the best place to build a house anywhere along the entire stretch of beach. The view was spectacular. The breeze blew all the time. "Well, Manuel. How about that? If I could have a lot anywhere, this would be the spot. If I can't afford the price, I can pick another lot."

Manuel looked at the place Andrew had marked. "Hmmm. I see you have chosen a very nice location. I am very familiar with that area. Yes. It is very nice. Very nice." He smiled at Andrew. "You are right. That cove is perfect for a small boat. Do you have a boat?" "Oh, no. Not yet. I thought I'd wait to see what happened first with getting a lot and how close to the cove it would be."

Manuel turned and pulled out a large book from the cabinet behind his desk and started searching through it. Finally, he stopped and seemed to peruse a page. "Ah. Yes. Here it is. The cost of the lot you have indicated. Hmmm."

Andrew closed his eyes and braced for an amount equaling the national debt. "Okay. I'm ready. But I already know I can't possibly afford it." He clenched his fist and cringed.

"Señor. Just a second. I need to check something. Please. It may take a few minutes." Manuel walked out of the office and was gone for almost twenty minutes. He returned, holding a file in his hand. As he walked to his desk, he was shaking his head and muttering. "Interesting. Very interesting. I apologize for taking so long. But it was very important. I had to be sure." He looked directly at Andrew. "If the family was to sell the lot at that location, the one you have indicated, it would cost ten thousand US dollars."

Andrew gasped, he was so shocked, his mouth fell wide open. "WHAT??!!"

"Ten thous…"

"Oh. Yes, I heard you, Señor Vargas. But are you sure? Ten thousand dollars?"

"Sí. Yes, Señor. Is something wrong?"

"Señor Vargas! THAT is an incredible price! Are you very sure it is correct? I cannot believe I could be so fortunate to purchase such a place for such a small amount." He looked directly at Manuel. "Really? Are you sure? Really?"

"Well. We can raise the price if you like." Manuel smiled and began to chuckle. "Just kidding. Just kidding. Yes. That is the correct price."

"Okay. Now, you are going to pull the rug out from under me and tell me the family isn't going to let me have it. I mean you did say IF the family were to sell the lot."

"Señor Andrew. I can have the papers drawn up for you by the end of the week. You can come and sign them. If possible, could you give us a check for a thousand dollars earnest money?"

Andrew was in total shock. He could hardly believe his ears. "Manuel! REALLY?? You're kidding! Really? I can have it?"

"Sí. Consider it yours. The paperwork will begin immediately. Sí. Yes." Manuel's eyes glinted. And with a huge grin on his face, he gave a great sigh. He sounded like a man, finally completing a mission long in the making. "We will also do the paperwork for placing it in a trust for you since you are not a citizen of the country."

Andrew looked up in the air and raised his arms up. "Thank you. Thank you. There is a God! I will write a check for the full amount. I had borrowed somewhat more, thinking I'd be paying big bucks for property near the beach. And here I am getting a lot ON the beach. It's more than I could have imagined or dreamed. And it's the lot I actually wanted. Yes! There is a God!"

Manuel smiled. "I am very glad you are happy. I will call you at your hotel when the papers are ready. I will also have a wonderful builder and architect meet you here that day. They are probably the best in the area if not the whole country for residential building."

"Manuel. What can I say? That would be great. I've been drawing plans for some time now for our retirement house. I studied architectural engineering and art in school. I can't believe it. I'm totally excited. Thank you so much. Gracias. Gracias. And know that when the house is finished, you must come for a visit."

After giving Andrew the name of an excellent boatbuilder located in Zihuatanejo, Manuel nodded. "I will see you later this week. And thank you for the invitation." He extended his hand and they shook. "Now, go buy that sailboat you were thinking about."

They both laughed.

Leaving Manuel's office, he headed directly to the boatbuilder's place. Andrew was very impressed with ones he saw that were in construction. He picked out the design he wanted and gave the man a check to cover the cost. The boat would be delivered and anchored in the cove in just a few months.

Andrew could hardly wait to send an email to Jacob, telling him of their extremely good fortune. He knew Jacob was not going to believe it.

Fate and Destiny had been waiting for this day. Little did Andrew realize but a long-awaited process had just begun, happening in Zihuatanejo.

That was in February 2004. After signing the paperwork, talking with the builder and the architect and reviewing the drawings, the house was soon started. It would be finished by that coming December or January. All agreed it was going to be spectacular.

There were several restrictions, regarding the property that had to be adhered to both during their life as well as after their death but he didn't care. They'd be dead. There was also a restriction, regarding resale. Sale would have to be back to the family again and at the fair market value at that time. Andrew knew they had no intentions of doing that. Selling was the farthest thing from their minds. He loved the spot and knew it would be the same for Jacob and they'd be there until they dragged their dead carcasses away.

Manuel indicated once the house was built and during the times no one was staying at the property, it would be maintained and kept up by their law firm. They would keep any vehicle at the law office complex, kept garaged there and running until someone returned again. That way they could be picked up at the airport in Zihuatanejo and have the vehicle all the while someone was visiting. Then, when ready to leave again, the vehicle would be taken to the offices prior to heading to the airport. The day or the time did not matter. It would be done.

The house was finished basically on schedule and Andrew and Jacob came down to move everything in by late February 2005. Much of Andrew's household things were packed and moved down. Even his piano as Jacob had bought him a new one to stay in Atlanta until they finally retired. At that time, he could sell the older one. The Jeep was brought down at that time as well. That year they spent just over two weeks unpacking and getting everything set up.

The sailboat was in the cove and ready to go. As indicated, the builder had brought it out and put it in the cove, anchor and all. A canvas cover was provided to keep the weather out of the boat. Jacob was ecstatic since he loved sailing. Andrew thought it strange a landlubber would be so enamored with a boat. But Jacob was and got to take the boat out numerous times before they had to return home again at the end of the month.

They also discovered a terrific photographer. He and his wife ran a small shop in Zihuatanejo and did excellent work. Andrew knew it would be great to use them for any special occasions in the future.

Andrew began to think of the next February, the February of 2006. No unpacking of boxes or getting the vehicle down. All that would be finished. All he and Jacob would have to do is just relax and enjoy all the peace and serenity. Jacob could sail out and get lobsters for them from the rock formations offshore if they wanted them. It was going to be amazing. So amazing.

Andrew stopped staring off into space and whispered. "Yes. It was going to be amazing." He shook his head and was silent for a moment. "That's what we thought. But who could have known?" He shook his head again and continued toward the beach.

CHAPTER III

So, here it was February 2006 and Andrew was here to relax, trying to cope and deal with memories. Alone. He walked down the bank. He turned his head to the right, looking north up the beach. Through the early light of dawn, he could see the waves hitting the rock formations out in the water. It also looked like the storm the night before had washed up some trash onto the beach. "Such a shame. People are such pigs." He quietly spoke and shook his head.

Slowly he turned his head to the left, observing the horizon beyond and the surf coming in toward him. He closed his eyes and breathed in the cool clean air. "It's not fair. Jacob should be here." Finally, he was looking south down the beach when he saw something large and dark right at the edge of the surf, down near the small cove. "Well. What has Mother Nature delivered here today?" He headed toward the object.

As he got closer, he could see it was not a big piece of driftwood or trash. It was the figure of a man in dark clothes. He had his right arm through a large life preserver. Andrew ran quickly toward the figure. "Oh, God! A drowned man on the beach! Holy crap! What can I do!?"

Reaching the man, Andrew saw he was still breathing and trying to move. "God give me strength." Andrew got down and grabbed the man and started to lift him up. It was not easy as the man was significantly bigger than he was and his clothes were saturated. But strangely, the man finally got to his feet with Andrew's help. Leaning on Andrew, they slowly started back to the house. All the while, he was giving encouraging words to the man that everything would be all right. Several times the man collapsed and Andrew had to help him back up again to continue onward.

Reaching the house, Andrew got him to the master bedroom and got him on the bed. There was a large cut on his forehead and he was mumbling incoherently. Andrew struggled to remove the wet jacket and shirt. He had to undo the jeweled cufflinks first. He set them on the nightstand. The jacket and shirt eventually came off. With great effort, he pulled off the leather boots, socks, the pants and undershorts. He noticed several bruises on the man's arms and legs probably from hitting the rocks coming to shore. He also had a thick, wide leather belt wrapped around his stomach with leather straps totally unrelated to his clothing. Andrew knew he had to remove it since it was wet through and through but he wouldn't open it. It was obviously something important, personal and private. He hung it on one of the chairs in the room to dry. He was also wearing a heavy gold rope chain around his neck with a large ornate gold cross encrusted with many jewels. There were several large rings on his hands.

"Damn. If the stones in those rings and cross are real, they're worth a king's ransom. Holy cow!" Andrew shook his head. "Good thing they didn't come off in the surf."

Running to the master bathroom, he got a large beach towel and started drying the man. His hairy legs and arms were first. Then, it was his stomach and chest that were also covered with thick black hair. His black, closely trimmed beard and mustache were done with care as was his thick, wavy black hair. All the while, the man continued making unintelligible sounds. The task completed, Andrew laid another towel over the man's naked midsection and placed a sheet over him.

He quickly got a facecloth to tend to the large wound on his head. He spoke softly. "Sorry, guy. I know the water isn't warm. Came from a bottle. Power's off and there's no hot water right now.

12

Sorry about that." Andrew spoke out of anxiety, knowing full well the man couldn't hear him.

It took some time but Andrew eventually got the man as comfortable as possible and placed some gauze over the wound on his head. He was exhausted. "I should make him some chicken soup in case he comes out of it and needs to eat something." He jumped up, went to the kitchen, opened a can from the pantry, used some bottled water and got it hot on the stove. He had to use a match since the built-in, electric spark on the stove was not working due to the power outage. He made periodic checks to make sure the man was still doing all right. The soup finally hot, he covered it, turned off the gas burner and returned to the bedroom, sitting in a chair next to the bed. That's when he had the time to really look at this handsome Neptune.

The light olive complexion made Andrew realize the man was Hispanic but not Mexican. His features were like Castilian heritage. To Andrew, he looked to be around his own age.

The man lay there quietly. His breathing appeared to be much better.

He placed a light blanket over the man to warm up his cold body even though the weather was warm outside.

When he hung the wet clothes in the master bathroom shower, Andrew could see the clothes were well-tailored and sophisticated. They were most likely evening clothes of a gentleman. The clothes of a man of wealth. "But what the hell was he doing, lying out there on the beach?" Then, he thought of the large life preserver. It was immediately obvious. "Damn! Did he fall off some flipping boat? Geez. Did a boat sink during the night? I'll bet someone's looking for him. Crap!"

Since the man was not waking up, Andrew put the soup in the fridge after it cooled, quickly closing the door. Returning to the room, he sat vigil through the day and the night, dozing on and off in the chair by the bed. He would light a candle now and then to enable him to see during his checks.

It was around nine o'clock the next morning when Andrew heard him stir. He stood up and looked at him. The man twisted in the bed and slowly opened his deep green eyes. He was looking right up at Andrew.

Andrew wanted to reassure him he was not in any danger. He spoke in a panic, gesturing all the while. "Señor. Hola, mucho guapo hombre amigo. ¿Cómo estás? Que tenga buen días. Mi español es mucho no bueno. Mucho poquito. ¿Habla inglés? ¿Por favor? ¿Cómo te llama? Mi tu amigo. Mi llama es Andrew." He shook his head. "Oh, shit! Why didn't I take Spanish in high school instead of French?" He pointed at himself with his right hand and gave a big smile.

The man looked hard at Andrew, braced himself with his arms, pulled himself up to a sitting position then leaned back on the pillows. His face showed expressions of anguish, seemingly to deal with the pain of the bumps and bruises. Finally, sitting up, he became relaxed. Looking right at Andrew, he slowly started to smile until his face was filled with an enormous grin. Then, he spoke in a deep yet soft voice, sounding much like that of Sam Elliott's. "You know. Your Spanish really needs a lot of work. A lot of work." He flexed his eyebrows several times and winked his right eye.

They both roared with laughter.

"Oh! Thank you, Jesus! You speak English! Thank you, God!" Andrew began clapping his hands and jumping up and down. He looked up in the air then back at the man. "I'm Andrew. Andrew Stevenson. And what's your name?" Andrew had a big smile on his face. "You had no wallet on you with your identification. It might have been lost at sea."

"Armando. Armando de Santiago." He looked down at his hands and his chest.

Andrew responded. "I had a feeling that belt was very important but it was soaked, so I took it off and hung it over here to dry." He pointed to the thick leather belt, hanging on the nearby chair. "I am so glad your rings and necklace didn't come off in the water.

They look rather expensive. And your cufflinks are over there on the nightstand."

"Oh. I was not concerned about that. I was just noticing. I am naked." He looked at Andrew and gave another big grin.

"Oh. Armando, your clothes were soaked. They're hanging in the shower to dry. I didn't want to put you to bed in wet clothes. I have to tell you, it wasn't easy getting them off, especially your boots. Those things are going to take forever to dry. I just hope the leather doesn't shrink. Now, how do you feel? You have a bad cut on your head and bumps and bruises all over you. We're going to have to watch that cut to make sure it doesn't get infected. We might even go see a doctor."

Armando reached up with his right hand to his forehead. "Thank you for taking care of me. Where am I? How did I get here?" He started looking around the room.

"I found you on the beach. But don't worry about that now. I have some chicken soup. I just have to heat it up. It'll be good for you. Forgive me. It's from a can. I promise I'll fix something better soon. I'm a pretty good cook. Would you like some hot tea or coffee?"

"Andrew. I would love to have some chicken soup. And some hot tea sounds very good right now. But could you help me into the water closet first?"

"Certainly. Here." Andrew assisted Armando up, wrapping the towel around him then to the bathroom. "You'll find some bottled water in the vanity under the sink." He opened the door to the cabinet under the sink. He pulled out a new toothbrush. "Here's a toothbrush for you to use and the toothpaste is next to the sink." He pointed at it. "If you need anything, let me know. If you want to take a shower, you can't right now. There's no water pressure and the water heater will not light. The power went out due to the storm. What can I say? You can use the toilet but you can only flush it once. I swear. The next purchase I make will be an LP generator." He left Armando and went to get the soup warmed up and make hot water

15

for tea. He yelled back as he headed to the kitchen. "Soup will be ready soon."

By the time Andrew had the soup and tea on a tray, taking it to the bedroom, Armando was coming out of the bathroom wrapped in his towel. Andrew placed the tray on the top of the dresser.

"I do feel better. I used some of the water to wet a cloth and wipe my face after I brushed my teeth. But I still feel a little unbalanced." Armando walked to the side of the bed. "May I put my rings and things here in this drawer? I will put my belt there when it dries." He pointed to the nightstand.

"Of course. Then, get in bed and I'll put the tray on your lap. Eat a little something then get some more rest. I'll check the cut later on when you finish eating and have your tea."

Armando placed the cufflinks and rings in the drawer but kept the cross around his neck. The thick belt would go in later. He got in bed.

"Before you rest, I want to change the dressing on that cut." Andrew went to the bathroom to get gauze and tape. "If you don't mind me asking, how the hell did you end up in the drink? It seems you must've fallen off a boat or it sank. Are there any others? I didn't see any more on the beach. Luckily, you made it to the beach. That was a rough storm last night. And it's so strange because it's not the rainy season."

Armando spoke softly as Andrew attended the cut. "I was sailing from Acapulco to San Francisco on a small freighter. Headed to get one of the family businesses started there. There was a horrible storm. I thought it was a hurricane. I was playing cards in the salon with some other passengers but needed to get some air. I went out on deck which I now know was an absolutely stupid idea in such a storm."

"Before I knew it, I got hit with a huge gust of wind. The railing gave way and I got blown over the side of the ship and into the ocean. Thank God, a crewman saw it happen. There was no way they could stop the ship and rescue me. There was no time and it was dark. They would never have been able to find me in the giant waves and darkness. The crewman grabbed a large life preserver from the wall of the ship and threw it out as far as he could to me. I guess he thought we were not that far from shore and maybe with a life preserver, I might make it there."

"Within minutes, the ship had disappeared in the darkness. I swam with all my might to get to the preserver. God was with me. If I had not grabbed it, I surely would have drowned. I hung on to it for dear life. It carried me off into the night. I have no idea how long I fought the waves. It was exhausting and I was tiring fast. Eventually, I realized I was near shore. I could hear the waves crashing against the rocks and the beach. I tried with all I had to get to the shore. As I did, I was tossed onto a huge rock, hitting my head. I stayed conscious just long enough to reach the beach where I passed out from pain and exhaustion. I remember nothing else. The next thing I remember is looking up and seeing you standing over me here in the bed." He smiled at Andrew.

Andrew continued to replace the bandages. "Well. Let me tell you. You must have a guardian angel. You're awfully damn lucky that crewman threw you a preserver. It probably saved your life. Along with being in as good a shape as you're in. Geez. If you'd been in my shape, you'd have been fish food." He gave a big grin. "Well, we can call whoever and let them know you're all right when you rest some more." He finished changing the gauze on the cut.

"It is not a problem. There is no rush to get to San Francisco. I think I deserve some time to rest up. It might be interesting to show up later with them thinking I am 'fish food' as you call it." He giggled.

Armando laid back to rest again. Finally asleep, he didn't wake through the entire day and into early evening.

Andrew lit a few candles as the light of day faded. That's when Armando woke up. Andrew looked at him. "I keep candles around. You never know when the electricity will go off. I'm going to fix you an omelet. It'll be light yet filling. I don't think you're quite ready for heavy food yet. I'll make more tea. I'll be in the kitchen.

"Andrew. Gracias. Thank you. I think I will get out of bed and eat in the dining room with you if you do not mind me sitting in a towel."

"Don't be ridiculous. If you are comfortable, that's all that matters. This place was built for fun and comfort, not stuffy formality. It's why we named it La Casa Sans Souci."

"Interesting. Mixing Spanish and French. I like it. La Casa Sans Souci. 'The house without worry.' Interesting." Armando sat down at the dining table in his towel. "I have to tell you. I have many questions. You said 'we' and you are obviously from the United States. But you are here in Mexico? Interesting. I do not hear or see anyone else in the house." He looked around the space. The kitchen was open to the dining room which was open to the living room, forming one large unobstructed area.

"And I see many artworks hanging on the walls." He got up and looked at the portrait of a man, hanging in the living room area. He saw the signature and date in the lower left-hand corner. "Hmmm. Interesting. You are a painter." He looked closer at the signature and date to make sure he was reading it correctly. He whispered to himself. "Yes. I did see that correctly. Very interesting." He did not say a word but immediately began to look around the room to see all that was there.

The candlelight cast a warmth to the interior. He began to observe everything in the room. He saw several framed pictures, standing on the tables and in the bookshelves. The figures in the pictures were the same as the ones on the dresser in the bedroom. He also noticed that one of the figures in the pictures had the face of the man in the portrait. He said nothing but his mind was beginning to form an opinion and idea of the man in the kitchen and what had happened.

At the far end of the living room, he saw a grand piano. "You will have to play for me sometime."

"Excuse me?" Andrew responded from the kitchen, not clearly hearing Armando.

"I see you play the piano. I love the piano. Will you play something for me sometime?"

"If you insist." Andrew giggled. "I really do need to replace the strings, though, with plated strings to keep them from rusting. This salt air is terrible on the piano. And as far as playing for you, I can do that if you don't mind some stumbling on the keyboard." Andrew paused briefly. "Please don't expect concert quality, you'll be sorely disappointed. Do you play?"

"No. Unfortunately. I never had the time. I was much too involved with the family business to take the time to learn."

"You know it's never too late. So says, my piano teacher. Now, you'll most likely never become another Horowitz or Ashkenazy but you'll be able to play some easier pieces for your own enjoyment and maybe for a few close friends who don't expect a Horowitz or an Ashkenazy. Hey. I didn't start till I was twenty-six. Yeah. Almost fourteen years ago. What can I say?"

"Now, if you had a guitar, I do play it a little."

"Really? I do have one in the closet in the bedroom. I'll get it for you after we eat. It'll need to be tuned, though. It's not been out of the case in ages. It was Jacob's. He replaced the strings with stainless steel ones, knowing we were coming here."

"I would like that." Armando clapped his hands. He heard exactly what Andrew said when he spoke the name of Jacob but did not pursue it. Maybe it would be a conversation for another time. As he watched Andrew's face when he spoke Jacob's name, there seemed to be some sign of pain. He realized that story wasn't going to have a good ending.

Just then, Andrew called out. "Okay! Soup's on! Have a seat. Now, remember. This is not the main dining room at the Ritz or Waldorf Astoria."

Armando sat down just as Andrew placed the plate in front of him. He poured the tea. "Sugar and lemon on the way." He returned

19

to the kitchen and got his plate, the sugar bowl and lemon wedges. After putting everything down, he got the flatware. Sitting down, he called out. "Okay. Dig in!" Andrew picked up his fork and started for the food on his plate when he saw Armando, bowing his head and crossing himself. He stopped quickly and waited. After a moment of silence, Armando crossed himself again and reached for his fork.

"I'm sorry. I apologize. It's been so long since I've said grace much less gone to Mass."

"It is all right. I just feel I owe the few moments to give thanks for all I have been given and how truly fortunate I have been in my life." He smiled at Andrew. "I was also giving thanks you were there on the beach to rescue me and help me from the sea. God has been kind to let such a man as you find me."

Andrew began to blush. Armando was so correct about giving thanks even with all that had happened in his own life. What was wrong with giving a few seconds of time to say thank you for all he DID have? Yes. There had been adversity but there had been many times of happiness and joy, too. Plus, he was successful in his business. "Yes. I totally agree. We'll say the blessing from now on. You're welcome but anyone who had found you would've done the same as me. By the way, I'm glad for the company. Thank you!" He looked at Armando and smiled.

"Your omelet is very good. Thank you. And no, you are wrong. Some would have seen me there, robbed me and just left me. But you took me home and cared for me. And all my things are still with me. I am glad to be in your company as well."

"I would've fixed toast but the toaster won't work with the power off. Sorry. And I can't light the oven for the same reason. It has an electric spark that lights it."

"Thank you for all you have done and are doing for me. Do not worry about things we have no control over." He smiled at Andrew and winked his right eye.

"I know. You're right."

Finishing up, Andrew removed the dishes and poured more tea. "If you're tired, please go rest. I'd love to sit and talk with you but it's important for you to get better and get rested. We can talk tomorrow. I'll get the guitar out and have it ready for you then."

"That would be great. I, too, want to talk with you but you are right. I feel a little unbalanced and I think I should get more rest."

"Then, to bed, my handsome Neptune. We'll talk tomorrow."

"Buenas noches, mi amigo. Hasta mañana." Armando smiled and winked his right eye. "Goodnight, my fine friend." He took the candle Andrew handed him to light the way.

Andrew blew out the candles in the room and took one to light his way to the third bedroom. This is where he would be sleeping as long as Armando was in the master bedroom. Tomorrow would be a day of discovery with his new friend from the sea.

CHAPTER IV

The next morning, Andrew got up and was pleased to see the electricity was back on. After hitting the guest bathroom, he headed for the kitchen to start breakfast. He didn't start the cooking as he wanted to wait for Armando to wake up. But he did get everything ready in preparation.

Shortly, he saw Armando come round the corner still with his towel wrapped around himself. "Armando. You can go take a shower now. There's water pressure. Shampoo and soap are in the shower. I'll wait until you're finished before we have breakfast. Oh. Yes. When I took your clothes off, I hung them in the shower. You can move them and put them on the back of the bathroom door. You've probably seen them there. You can also flush the toilet."

"A shower would be very nice." He turned and went back into the bedroom. After a while, he appeared again and wrapped in a towel. "I feel much better. Thank you. I did put the clothes on the hooks on the bathroom door. They are dry."

Andrew looked at Armando, standing there. "Not to worry. I see we're going to have to get you some new clothes. I don't think you want to keep running around in a towel all day long. I mean, I wouldn't mind but hey. And it's quite obvious mine would be way too small." He clapped his hands. "Since the electricity's back on, I fixed coffee. Would you like some?"

"Yes. Yes, I would."

"Would you like sugar and cream? I have some great hazelnut creamer. I love it."

"That sounds wonderful. Yes. Some hazelnut creamer."

"If you use the creamer, taste it before you put sugar in it. The creamer may make it sweet enough." Andrew poured two mugs of coffee with creamer and handed one to Armando. "How is it?"

Armando took a sip. "This is very good. Very good. Thank you. I like it. Gracias. And you are right. It needs no sugar." Armando went and sat at the dining table.

As Andrew came to the table with his coffee, he flipped the switch to the chandelier over the table. The lighting of the fixture seemed to startle Armando. He almost dropped his mug as he looked up.

"Oh, Andrew. I guess I am still a little unbalanced." He stared intensely at the fixture.

"Okay. After some ham and eggs and toast, we're going to run into town and get you some new clothes. Your clothes are dry but not sure about your boots. We'll get you some sneakers first. Too bad I don't have some of Jacob's things here. You might've been able to get into some of his." He gave a sad smile.

After breakfast, Armando dressed in his clothes and boots. The boots were not easy to get on as they were still a little wet.

They walked out to the garage and Andrew went to the driver's side of the Jeep. He looked at Armando. "Come on. Get in. And don't forget to buckle up." He climbed into the driver's seat.

Armando climbed into the passenger seat and looked over at Andrew, buckling his seat belt. He did the same.

"Okay. You ready?" Andrew stuck the key in the ignition, turned it and the engine started up.

Armando seemed a bit apprehensive but finally settled in and observed as Andrew backed the Jeep up and headed down the drive. He didn't say much during the forty-five-minute ride into Zihuatanejo. He was more interested in everything around him. He didn't mind the breeze in the open vehicle.

Finally, they arrived. It was a place Andrew knew well. The store sign had a big pelican on it. He knew you could get everything from soup to nuts there. If they couldn't get it there, they could go to the SAM'S store.

As they got out of the Jeep, Armando looked at Andrew and then at the Jeep. "This thing sure does go fast."

"Hey! It's a Jeep!" Andrew gave a big grin.

Walking toward the store, many stopped and looked at Armando. Armando realized it was his evening clothes. And here it was late morning.

Entering the store, people continued staring at Armando and his attire. They headed into the shoe department.

Andrew saw a young lady who worked in the store. "Hola, Señorita. My friend needs a new pair of sneakers and some sandals."

Andrew was so pleased that many of the stores in Zihuatanejo had employees who spoke English. It was probably due to the fact that Zihuatanejo and Ixtapa were major tourist destinations for many Americans.

"Certainly, Señor. Come this way." She looked Armando up and down. "What happened to your friend's head?"

"He had a very bad accident. But he is fine now. Thank you for your concern." Andrew smiled at her.

"It looks like he may need some clothes, as well." She giggled and led the way. "What size shoe does he wear?"

"You're so right there." Andrew agreed. Then, he looked at Armando. "Okay. What size shoe do you wear?"

Armando looked puzzled. "I do not know. My shoemaker measures my feet and makes my boots and shoes." He shrugged his shoulders.

Andrew looked at the saleslady. "I think he needs around a ten or eleven. Blanco." He turned to Armando. "Oh. Geez. I'm sorry. They're for you. I guess you should have some say in this."

Armando grinned. "Well. Since I have no money right now and you are buying, you pick them out. I know you will get something satisfactory. Blanco is just fine."

The young lady left then returned with a pair of size ten white sneakers as well as a pair of sandals that looked perfect.

Armando struggled to remove one of his boots. "I think you are right. The leather must have shrunk." After some coaxing, the boot came off. He set it down and started putting on the sneakers. "It feels tight."

"One moment, Señor." She took his boot and went away but was back shortly. "These are a little bigger. Try and see if it is better. I compared the bottom of his boot with the sole of the sneakers and the sandals. And here are a few pairs of socks for you."

Armando removed his old ones and put on a pair of white athletic socks and one of the sneakers. "Oh. Mejor. Better. Much better. Gracias."

"Take off your other boot and put on the other one, so you can walk around a bit." Andrew was insistent.

Armando removed his other boot and sock and put on the new sock and sneaker. He walked around the area. "Yes. These feel very good and comfortable. I like them. Sneakers." He gave a big smile.

"Señor. You wear a size twelve." She smiled. "Now, try the sandals."

Armando took off the sneakers, slipped the sandals on and walked around. "They are wonderful. Thank you."

Andrew got his wallet and pulled out his credit card, handing it to the young lady. "I think he should wear them now. Could we have another bag for his boots?"

"Certainly, Señor. Come this way to a register up front."

"We are going to get him some clothes, too. Can we get them before going to the register?"

"Of course. We can do it all together when you are ready. What else are you looking for?"

"He needs some jeans, shirts, T-shirts, underwear, some shorts. And a nice wallet. Let me see. What else? Oh, yes. A bathing suit. One of those boxer styles."

"Right this way, Señor." She led them to the men's department. "What size jeans and shirt?"

Andrew looked questioningly at Armando. "Don't tell me. You have no idea because you have all your clothes done by your tailor." He bent his head down shaking it, trying not to snicker.

"Señor. You look like you might wear a thirty-six long and a thirty-three waist. Here you go." She picked out a pair and handed them to Armando. "Just one moment and I will get you some underwear. I have a feeling your friend wants you to wear them now. There is a fitting room right around here." She led Armando to the room.

Andrew called out. "If they fit, she's right! Leave them on! You can wear them." He turned to the saleslady. "Do you have a few bags we can carry his clothes in?"

She smiled. "Not a problem, Señor. And I will go with you to the front register to explain to the clerk there."

Armando called out. "She is correct. These fit very well."

"Stay in there. We're going to find you a shirt to see if it'll fit. And also a bathing suit and some shorts." He smiled at the young clerk. "What do you think?"

"I am sure he would wear a large shirt with probably a sixteen collar. This way. We can get a bathing suit first."

After finding a nice bathing suit and a couple of shorts, they headed to the shirts. Andrew picked out three shirts. One had long sleeves and the other two had short sleeves along with some T-shirts. He held the short-sleeved one up and turned to the saleslady. "How do you think this will look on him?"

"Señor. I think your friend will look very handsome in any shirt he wore." She had a big smile on her face. "And if it fits, we have some very nice Guayaberas you might want to see."

"Excellent. I might even get myself one or two. Thank you." They headed back to the dressing room and Andrew handed the shirt to Armando. "Let me know how this works."

After a few moments, his reply came from the dressing room. "It is perfect. Not as fitting as the shirts my tailor makes for me but very nice." He started to laugh out loud. Andrew and the young lady joined in the laughter. Finally, he stepped out fully dressed in his new clothes and sneakers. "Well. What do you think?"

"Señor. You look very nice. Very handsome." She raised her hands as if in prayer with a big smile.

"Belt! He needs a belt." Andrew blurted out. They picked out a nice leather one for Armando to wear as well as a leather wallet.

"But Andrew. I have nothing to put in the wallet."

"Don't worry. You never know what you may pick up you can put in it." He turned to the young lady. "Could we see the Guayaberas? I can see he'll look fantastic in one."

After a while, they gathered everything they needed in the men's department and headed to the front register. The young lady was extremely helpful in explaining and giving the clerk the price tags for all the items. They thanked the young lady for all her help. On their way out, Andrew also picked up a bag of charcoal for the grill.

The next stop was the liquor store. Makings for Bloody Marys, Gin and Tonics, Margaritas and Whiskey Sours were on the list. A few bottles of red and white wines completed the supply. Then, it was home.

Armando spoke as they got out of the Jeep with the bags of goodies. "Thank you so much for doing all this. I will pay you back one day. I promise."

"Don't be silly. You needed some clothes. It's nothing. Maybe one day you can have your tailor make me a new suit." He looked right at Armando with a huge grin on his face.

"Andrew. I am a bit tired. Would you mind if I got a little rest?"

"No sweat. I have to get a few things done in the kitchen. Going to make up a batch of Bloodys, Whiskey Sours and Margaritas. Will have them on hand in the fridge. We can have some later on after you get up."

When Armando woke up and came into the dining room, it was almost six in the evening. Andrew had soft music playing on the CD player. "How was your rest?"

"I slept very well. Thank you."

"By the way. I got the guitar out of the closet. It's on the piano bench." Andrew went and turned off the music.

Armando headed to the far end of the living room. He looked down at the black case. There was a brass plaque on the lid. Words were engraved on it.

JACOB
You are the light in my life…
You are the music in my heart.
Forever your friend,
Andrew
Christmas 1998

He paused a moment, looking hard at what he read and the date before opening the case. He whispered to himself. "I cannot imagine how this has happened." His face grimaced and he shook his head. Then, he opened the case. There, lying in a bed of black felt, was a beautiful classical guitar. "This looks like a very nice guitar." He picked it up and strummed it. "You are right. It does need some tuning." He started adjusting the keys to get the strings in tune. After a little while, he was satisfied with the sound and began a little Flamenco-sounding music.

"Hey! That sounds really good. Keep playing. In case you're wondering, we are having pollo frito tonight."

"That sounds good to me. Can I help in any way?"

"I have it under control. Dinner in about an hour. Would you like a drink? Bloody Mary? Margarita? Gin and Tonic? Whiskey Sour? We'll have wine with dinner."

"How about a Margarita? That sounds good."

"Margarita it is."

During dinner, there was little said. Afterward, they went to the living room and sat down for more meaningful conversation.

Andrew jumped right in. "Well. Obviously, from your tailored clothes, your specially made boots, your expensive rings and necklace, you're NOT from the poor side of town." Andrew bent his head, trying not to laugh. "I'm sorry. I couldn't help it. So, what do you do to keep yourself busy?"

"I am so glad you find this so amusing." He grinned and winked his right eye. "Let me see if I can summarize it all." He took a sip of his Margarita. "The family goes all the way back to Europe. Spain. Middle Ages. It became one of the 'well-to-do' in banking and jewelry. Our family became known for its fine jewelers and its fairness in banking and finance. Over the centuries, the family became rather wealthy."

"I am the oldest of three sons. I went to school in England." He glanced at Andrew. "That is how I know English. Yes. I am still in banking and precious stones. The rings and cross I have were made by my finest jeweler. I keep my cross on me as it is really special. It was blessed by the Pope."

"My parents came to Mexico…" He paused for a moment, quickly figuring out how to continue. "A long time ago and settled in Acapulco. They are now gone." He crossed himself. "I live there now and use it as my base. My youngest brother lives in Madrid and heads up the jewelry end of our family business. He likes the big city. My middle brother lived in New York until…" He paused again. "Until recently but has gone to San Francisco. He likes the opportunities it offers. I was headed there to help get things organized and off the ground with our business there. He is quite capable of doing it all by himself but thought 'Big Brother' might like to pitch in. Sometimes I travel for them, checking on gem mines, collateral for investments, clients. They are married but I am not. By me doing the footwork, it allows them to stay home with their families." Armando gave a big smile and looked at Andrew. "Now, it is your turn."

"Hey. Ah. Not so fast. What about that someone special? No mention of one."

"There is no special 'one' as you call it. I have been so busy and just never met anyone who made me interested."

"Okay. You have to be kidding. A handsome man like you and there hasn't been anyone? What can I say? I know there's no reason for you to be dishonest with me. But damn. Interesting. I guess you have to watch out for gold diggers. With your obvious money, I'll bet women flock out of the woodwork."

Andrew paused a moment then questioned again. "What about things you like to do. Like your guitar playing. Is there anything else?"

"Not really. I do appreciate literature, art and music, though I am not one who produces it. I do like sailing and fishing. Hunting is all right but I really do not enjoy killing animals. That is it. Really." He looked at his empty glass. "Would it be possible to have another one of these? They are very good. I love lime."

"Okay. I guess I'll let you off the hook for now." Andrew gave a big grin. "I may have more questions later. I'll tell you. Since you like sailing, I have a small boat anchored down in the cove but I think it's way too early for that right now."

He took Armando's glass and refilled it from the fridge. He refreshed his own. Coming back, he handed him the drink before sitting down and began his tale.

"I grew up in Virginia. In the States. Old Virginia family, going back to sixteen twenty near Jamestown. There was a plantation just south of Richmond but we lost it in the 'Recent Unpleasantness'. That's how I refer to the Civil War." Andrew grinned. "Now. Middle-class family. Oldest of four. Two brothers and a sister. Went to college in Virginia. Go Hokies!" He thrust his right fist up into the air. "Studied art and architecture. Had a great time. Met some really nice folks there."

"Moved to Atlanta after graduating and was an engineer for a while but they got rather nosy about my life. Left them and started my catering company. Been pretty successful with it. My big thing there are the cakes. Have had recognition for some of my confectionery work. I enjoy it and it affords me what I have. I paint, play the piano a little. Back in college, I did play the guitar and the E-flat alto saxophone back in grade school. I'm a pretty good cook. There. That about does it." He looked at Armando and smiled.

"Aaahhh. I do not think so." He looked around the room at the portrait and many framed photographs everywhere then back at Andrew. "I think there is a lot more. Who is he? He looks very important to you. Is he the 'we' of whom you have spoken and whose guitar I have played?"

Andrew turned to the portrait. "Jacob." He seemed to stare into the painting and spoke softly. "Jacob and I were… good friends, best friends." He took a drink and looked down into the glass. "He died. In a fire. Last May."

There was a long silence before Armando spoke. "Andrew. I am sorry. I can see it on your face. This is something very hurtful, painful and close to you. I did not mean to bring up bad things."

"No. It's all right. I have to learn to cope with it. If you want, I'll tell you about him. I also want to warn you. In doing so, I will be telling you something about myself with which you may not be comfortable."

"Please. Tell me. I do not think there is anything you could tell me that would make me think poorly of you. I have seen how kind and caring you are. I see you are a good person. What could be so bad?"

"Armando. Telling you about Jacob involves a rather long story to explain. If you want to know it, I'll tell you but let's wait until tomorrow. Maybe we can go walk on the beach in the morning and then come back here and I'll tell you all about him."

"That sounds good. I think I need to get more rest anyway. Our trip to town was somewhat fatiguing. You are right. Tomorrow would be better."

As Armando headed to the master bedroom, Andrew called out. "If you need anything, let me know. Extra towels and stuff are in the closet in the bathroom. Oh. One thing." He came into the bedroom. "The ceiling fan is remote. You have to use this control to work it." He showed the way to change the speeds and how to turn it on and off. "There you go. You may not need the fan with the breeze coming in off the mountains. But just in case." He turned and started out of the room.

"Andrew. Thank you so much for your kindness and goodness. I truly appreciate all you have done for me. Goodnight and see you in the morning."

"Armando. Thank you. You're more than welcome. That's what friends are for. I think we're going to become really good friends." He nodded and smiled.

Armando looked back and smiled, winking his right eye. "Yes. I know we are going to be great friends."

CHAPTER V

Andrew was up early and started breakfast before Armando got up. He had all preparation done for French Toast when Armando walked into the dining room. He was wearing the pale blue boxer bathing suit and sandals bought the day before. "How's your head today? We need to change those bandages again before we eat."

"Okay. Very good." Armando agreed.

Finishing the change of bandages, they headed back into the dining room again. Andrew went to the kitchen and Armando sat at the table.

"I thought I would put on the bathing suit you bought for me since you said we were going to walk on the beach. Is it not appropriate?" Armando tipped his head to the side.

"We were both thinking the same thing. I have mine on, too. Most appropriate but we're going to bring towels, so we don't get sunburned. And speaking of sunburn, I have some sunscreen in the cabinet under the sink. I'll get it. It has a high rating to prevent major burn. We can put it on after we eat. I hope you like French Toast. I fix it the way it is supposed to be fixed. Not covered with pancake syrup but with butter, sugar and cinnamon. I don't know who thinks pancake syrup was made for French Toast. It was made for pancakes. Oh duh!! Here. I fixed you a mug of coffee, too."

With eating over, they smeared the sunscreen on, filled their mugs with more coffee and headed to the beach. The sun was bright and the breeze was great.

Andrew looked up at the sky. "Even though we have sunscreen, we can't stay out too long. But you already know that, being from Acapulco."

"Yes. But I did not get the chance to just stroll on the beach very much. And when I did, I was alone. This will be fun."

"I've always believed a fun time should be shared with a friend when possible." Andrew ran down to the beach in front of Armando. Suddenly, he turned around. "I don't see the preserver from the ship. I guess the tide took it back out. Thought you might have liked to keep it as a souvenir. Oh, well. I have an idea. Let's build a sandcastle. Damn. I need to go back to the house and get some things to help do it."

"A sandcastle?"

"Sure. Why not! Wait here. I'll be right back. Give me your coffee mug and I'll refill it." Andrew ran to the house and shortly returned with a small bucket, containing a dinner knife and two large spoons. The bucket handle was on his arm and a mug of coffee in each hand. "We can do a small one today. Let's see how the sand holds up." He handed Armando his mug.

"Where should we do this?" Armando looked up and down the beach.

"Right down in front of the house. That way we can watch it when the tide comes in and washes it away." Andrew chuckled.

"All right. If you insist. But I do not understand why you should want to build something only to watch it be destroyed by the tide." Armando shook his head and took a sip of coffee.

Andrew raised his eyebrows and a big grin filled his face. "It's called 'temporary art'."

After about two hours, Andrew spoke up. "The sand hasn't been too stable here. I thought we could do something more detailed but not if the sand isn't stable. Oh, well. We at least tried." He stood back and looked at the strangely shaped pile of sand. "What can I say?" He looked up at the sun. "We need to get out of the sun before we turn into crispy critters."

Armando gave a weird look. "Turn into what?"

"Crispy critters. Things cooked so much they get crispy. You know. Like the pollo frito I made."

Armando tilted his head back. "Oh. All right. If you say so. But before we do, I want to get in the water." He handed his mug to Andrew and headed to the surf.

Before Andrew could respond about the bandage on his head, Armando was into the surf, diving into a wave that was coming ashore. When he returned to the surface, he called out. "The water is nice. Come on in."

"All right. But come over here first. Your bandage is coming off." He set the mugs down on the sand.

Armando walked over to Andrew and stood in front of him. Andrew looked at the bandage, half hanging off. "You know. I think the saltwater would do it good." He removed the bandage completely. "There. And it's looking a lot better today." Then, he looked right up into Armando's face with a big Cheshire Cat grin. "Last one in is a rotten egg!" Andrew ran toward the surf. Armando was right behind him.

After splashing around for a little while, they got out, dried off, gathered everything and headed up to the house.

They wiped the sand off their feet before entering the house. "Andrew. That was so refreshing. I cannot believe how much fun it was. I would never have done such a thing by myself."

"Yes, it was. We'll do it again. I'm glad we got in the water. I knew it should be warm but wasn't sure. It really was nice." He paused for a moment and smiled as he looked off into space. "Jacob loved the beach." There was another moment of silence before he continued. "I need to get this wet bathing suit off before I do anything else." He headed to the third bedroom where he was sleeping since he let Armando have the master bedroom.

"I agree. I will put on a pair of the shorts you got for me." Armando headed to the master bedroom.

Soon, they both emerged. Andrew went to the kitchen and Armando went to the living room.

"I know it's still a little early but not for me. How about a Bloody Mary? When I visit my sister, we start them around eight in the morning." He pulled the jug out of the fridge and shook it vigorously. Two large glasses from the cabinet were soon rimmed with lime, dipped in Cajun seasoning, filled with ice, several olives, a stalk of celery, a long slice of cucumber, a wedge of lime and almost to the rim with the mixture from the jug. He carried them into the living room and handed one to Armando. "I never asked if you liked them. If not, don't worry. I can fix you a Margarita."

Armando took his glass and sipped. "Excellent. This is very good. If all your drinks are like the ones I have had so far, you should have a saloon." He smiled and winked his right eye.

"Hey. The catering business is tough enough." He raised his glass to Armando and looked at him. "To a newfound friend. Literally."

Armando raised his glass. "Yes. To a new friend… who found me."

They both chuckled and slapped their knees.

After a moment, he looked at Andrew, at the portrait of Jacob then back at Andrew. "I hope you do not mind me prying but I am very interested in hearing about you and Jacob."

Andrew looked hard at Armando. "If I'm to tell you about Jacob, there's something I have to tell you so you'll understand."

Armando looked around the room at the several photographs. "I had a sense there was more to you both than just a friendship. I can see it on your faces in the pictures. There is happiness there. There is love."

Andrew was silent for a moment, turned to the painting then back to Armando. "I met Jacob by accident. Talk about the Fates stepping in. It was not long after I moved to Atlanta. Right after college. A friend of mine dragged me out one Friday evening to a bar. I really didn't want to go but he was insistent. I thought, what the hell, so I went."

"We walked through the dimly lit room to the far side and stood at the shelf along the wall. My friend left and went to get us each a cocktail. As I turned around, I saw a man sitting and leaning back against the main bar. He was dressed in his jeans, flannel shirt open to his beltline, exposing his chest covered with thick black hair and a cowboy hat set back on his head of black wavy hair. Needless to say, I couldn't stop looking at him. I watched his face. He had such a great smile when he talked with the others around him."

"My friend soon returned with our drinks and blurted, 'There's a guy I want you to meet at the bar.' He grabbed my arm."

"Strangely, we started walking in the direction of the man I'd been looking at. My mind was surprised my friend would know this man. Seemingly, in an instant, there we were, standing in front of him. He looked up at my friend and spoke. 'Hey, Larry. How are you? And who is this with you?' He turned and looked up at me."

"Larry spoke. 'Jacob. This is Andrew.'"

"I got so flustered, I reached out with my hand and rubbed it across Jacob's chest. At the same time, I spoke. 'Look at that nice furry chest.' My whole body went into a state of shock and embarrassment. Suddenly, my whole being wanted to disappear into oblivion. I could hear the words screaming out in my head. 'You IDIOT! What have you done?'"

"But before I could pull my hand back, he grabbed it and held it tight against his chest. He looked into my eyes and smiled. 'Cold hands. Warm heart.'"

"I have no idea what I said or actually did after that. I do know he was kind to me and I knew somehow I had to see him again."

"Sometime the next week, I asked Larry if he knew how to get in contact with Jacob. He was obliging, not only giving me his phone number but telling me about him."

Andrew looked over at Armando and got up. "Here. Give me your glass. I'll get us both another." Within minutes he was back, resuming his story.

"Yes. Jacob was a fireman but on the side, he was a landscaper. Firemen work twenty-four hours on then forty-eight hours off. During those forty-eight hours, he did landscaping. He truly loved his landscape work."

"I also found out he didn't live very far away from me. I have to tell you, I was so afraid to call him. Good looks have always intimidated me and I thought Jacob was so handsome." Andrew glanced over at the painting before continuing. "But I finally got up the courage. When I told him who I was, I knew he was being kind in telling me he remembered me." He shook his head. "Strangely, it wasn't until years later I found out he really did remember me. He told me no one, not anyone, had ever had the brass to do what I did to him at the bar. He had considered calling me because he liked guys who were uninhibited and did what they felt like doing at the time."

"Over time, we periodically saw one another. It wasn't long until we knew there was something more than just friendship. He wanted me to move in with him but I had reservations, regarding his job. He'd always kept his private life private, not wanting anyone to know he was a homosexual. If we lived together, that secret would become obvious. Since we each had our own homes and after much conversation, we decided I was right. But it didn't mean we wouldn't stay over with one another. A few days at his place and a few at mine. The structure or place didn't matter. We were together."

"Yes. We had a slightly unconventional relationship but it worked. Jacob told me even though we didn't live together, it didn't matter because he knew I cared and loved him." Andrew watched Armando to see his expression. He was surprised. There was no shock on his face like he expected. He continued.

"Jacob and I shared many, many great times together." Andrew looked up in the air and snickered. "There was one thing Jacob loved. 'Rubbies' as we called it. He liked me to give him back and body rubs. I remember this one time I was over at his house, doing some work there. He began to moan a bit with a sad look on his face and reached round at his back, telling me his back hurt and ached. I looked right at him and asked if he wanted some 'rubbies'. He immediately flashed a huge grin and his face lit up like a kid on Christmas morning. Then, he ran out of the room. I knew where he was going. I finished up what I was doing and headed into his bedroom. There he was. Sprawled out on the bed. Naked with a big grin on his face. All I could do was shake my head. Those were the days."

"Then, came that Friday morning, May the thirteenth, last year." He paused for a moment in thought. "Yeah. Friday the thirteenth. Wooooo. What can I say? I was organizing everything for a major catering job that evening. I wanted everything to be right, so nothing could go wrong. After all, it WAS Friday the thirteenth."

"The phone rang. It was Jacob's cousin calling to tell me there had been a major fire the previous night. 'Andrew, it was horrible. The roof collapsed on some of the men. Everyone got out except one.' Then, there was a moment of silence before she spoke again."

Andrew paused for a moment, staring out into space before he began again. He spoke softly. "And then, came the words. Those three words still sting, piercing my body and mind... my soul. I can close my eyes and I hear them as clearly as if they were just spoken. 'Jacob is dead.' I screamed out and dropped the phone, crying incessantly. The loving, caring and kind man I knew was gone. My Jacob was dead. Never to return. The plans we'd made. Gone. Jacob had been designing the landscaping for the house here. The life we imagined. Our plans for eventual retirement here in Mexico. All was wiped away in one fell swoop."

"What I couldn't understand is he wasn't scheduled to work that day. We had talked about it sometime before. We even joked about it being Friday the thirteenth. It's strange. Jacob said he had met this guy who came into the restaurant where he used to go eat all the time. This had happened on several occasions. The guy told him he should not work on that day and made him promise. Jacob thought it kind of freaky but the guy seemed to be a nice and friendly person, so he took his advice and requested to be off that shift. But wouldn't you know it? I found out later, one of the other guys had a family situation come up and Jacob said he'd fill in for him. Jacob most likely saved the life of the guy who was married and had three kids."

"People don't understand. They don't get it. They keep telling me 'time heals all pain' and 'you need to move on with your life'. That's total bull crap. When you love someone, you just don't sweep them and all you had with them out the door and start anew overnight. And here it is almost a year later and I still love him and miss him. I know I always will, no matter what happens." Andrew looked at his glass. "I need another." He looked at Armando.

Armando answered quietly. "Yes. Please. Thank you."

When Andrew returned, he handed Armando his glass then sat down.

Armando spoke quietly. "I am so sorry. I know it was devastating. I can tell now. I see your heart is broken to pieces. Seeing all the pictures, the portrait and now, hearing the story makes it so clear how much you loved Jacob. Thank you for telling me. I believe you are going to love Jacob as long as you are alive. I will also tell you and I mean no disrespect but should another man come into your life, I think he will understand. And the love you share with him will not diminish the love you will always have for Jacob, nor will it diminish the love you will have with him. I will also tell you. This conversation has made me understand something I have been wondering about and dealing with for many years."

Andrew shook his head and showed an expression of surprise. "What do you mean?"

"I have been living a double life. I have always known I was not like my brothers. I never was attracted to women. Even beautiful women. Yes. I can appreciate them and enjoy their company and friendship but I have never had a physical attraction toward them. As long as I can remember, I have had an eye for men. Unlike you and Jacob, I have never been able to act on these feelings. I have never been able to discuss it with anyone, knowing the thinking of everyone I know, regarding such an alliance. I have been so afraid. I was afraid of rejection by those I love. I have seen how men like that are treated, should they be discovered. I have been afraid of being condemned by the church. You are the first man I have ever told about this." He took a deep breath. "Being who I am and the position I have in society has made it impossible to even attempt to act on my feelings. But hearing your story and being able to tell you, I feel so much better. I feel as if a huge weight has been lifted off me. Can you understand what I am trying to tell you?"

Andrew was taken totally by surprise. "Holy cow. Geez. Wow. Armando. I must tell you about something that happened to me. I was also afraid even being with Jacob. I was afraid how friends and family would react. I don't know how it came to be but someone told me I needed to talk with a certain priest." He looked hard at Armando. "Yes. A priest. So, I took his advice and made an appointment with this priest."

"I went to visit him. When the door opened, there was a big bear of a man, dark wavy hair, beard and mustache. And what a great huge smile he had on his face. I immediately felt a sense of caring and warmth. He invited me in and we sat down and talked. It was incredible. He was a totally understanding and helpful man. He constantly kept telling me I was a child of God. God made me and God doesn't make mistakes. But there was one thing he told me that really hit the nail on the head. I have told many about it. It was a comparison."

"There are two men. Man 'A' and man 'B' from different backgrounds, education and thinking. Now, what you have to understand here is, you cannot lie to yourself. You know the way you truly feel. If you believe you have done wrong, you KNOW you have done wrong. Now, keep that in mind. Okay. Both men commit the same act. They do exactly the same thing. Man 'A' believes he's done wrong. In the eyes of God, he has done wrong. Man 'B', on the other hand, doesn't believe he's done wrong. In the eyes of God, he has done no wrong. Regardless of what society or the religious say, if you truly believe you are doing no wrong in something you do, you have done no wrong. Now, remember this. You must believe it totally in your heart and soul. You must not lie to yourself."

"Well, when I heard this, to say I was astounded, would be an understatement. And what I was hearing was coming from a priest. I have always believed God is not a petty God but totally understanding and made us the way we are for reasons. I think I was made this way so I might understand what it is like to know discrimination."

"Then, I told him I hadn't been to communion in so long because I'd not gone to confession. He looked right at me with a big smile and said. 'Have you murdered anyone lately?' I was so shocked, we both just roared with laughter. He continued. 'God doesn't care about stupid ridiculous stuff. What God cares about is have you murdered anyone lately.'"

"When I left that afternoon, I felt incredibly amazed. What can I say?"

"A priest told you that? A priest said that? What a wonderful man! How understanding. That is amazing. Incredible! What you have told me has changed my whole life! Yes, it is true I may have to hide what I feel and know about myself but there will no longer be those feelings of self-hate and shame. Especially, when I do not believe I should have those feelings. I wish I could know this man. He is the kind of man we need leading the church."

Andrew responded. "I believe one day there will be such a man who will become Pope and talk against the ridicule and misunderstanding about many things the church has always considered wrong. Something tells me you'll have to read a favorite book of mine. It's called The Road Less Traveled. There's a wonderful statement in the book. It goes something like this: 'To be bigoted is easy. It only takes ignorance. To become enlightened is very difficult because it may mean you might have to change some of your fundamental thinking.'"

"You know." Armando smiled. "That is so true. I think about the belief back in the fourteenth century about the world being flat and the world being the center of the universe. It was the truth of the day. Well, that changed through enlightenment. Columbus and Magellan proved the world was round and Galileo and Copernicus showed the world was NOT the center of the universe. Those who kept believing what was taught in the past were continuing to live in ignorance."

Andrew spoke out. "Exactly."

"Regardless of where I go, people recognize me and I have always known it would be impossible for me to act on my feelings. It could never be kept a secret. But here with you, I do not have to hide. There is no one here who will question, criticize or judge me. Out there, I will still have to hide my inner self out of respect for my family and position. But knowing there is someone who has talked with me about this, has been an enormous help and lifted a huge burden from my soul. You know, something tells me even though getting here was traumatic, I think God allowed it, so I could meet you."

"Let's not stretch things too far." Andrew took a sip of his drink. "But I do believe the Fates sometime step in to guide and help people. I have always believed things happen for reasons and we meet the people we do for reasons. Some reasons may be small but some are large and have a huge impact. Yes. Now, let's go take another walk on the beach. Go get a long sleeve shirt on, so you don't burn. I will, too."

"May I wear one of the Guayaberas you bought me?"

"Of course. Go put one on. When we get back, I'll fix us something to eat."

"Can I get a refill before we go?" Armando held up his glass with a huge smile.

Andrew called out. "Give me that glass."

They walked for several hours up and down the beach just enjoying the warm sun and the sound of the crashing surf. The sun was well below the horizon when they got back and Andrew fixed dinner. Afterward, they went into the living room to listen to some easy listening music on the CD player.

After a while, Armando looked at Andrew. "Play something for me."

"Really? You want me to play?"

"Please. Por favor."

Andrew got up, turned off the CD player and sat on the piano bench. "I'll play three of my favorite classical pieces for you. Two of them were written by Debussy and the third by Rachmaninoff: *Clair de Lune*, the *Premiere Arabesque* and the *Eighteenth Variation* from the *Rapsody on a Theme of Paganini*. Please, forgive the bumbles and mistakes."

After playing the final chord of the third piece, he smiled and was rather surprised at how well he'd played them.

"That was beautiful. Really beautiful. Please, play one more. Por favor."

"Okay. One more. From the Classics to a more recent classic." He looked into Armando's face. "This one is especially for you." He gave him a big smile and pointed at his eyes. "I don't have the best voice but I'll sing it anyway. It's a song Rosemary Clooney used to sing and made famous called *Green Eyes*. I loved the way she sang it." After a moment, he began, starting with a slow introduction. "'Your green eyes with their soft lights, your eyes that promise sweet nights…'" Andrew kept playing and singing to the end. "'All through my life they'll taunt me. But will they ever want me? Green eyes… I love you.'" After the sound of the piano faded, he looked over at Armando. "So. I apologize to Rosemary Clooney for not doing her wonderful song justice."

"I loved it." Armando clapped his hands in applause. "I would like for you to play it again for me sometime." Armando smiled and winked his right eye.

"Yeah. You and your green eyes. I just know they could get you into a lot of trouble. Especially, with that handsome face of yours. Oh, yeah."

Armando spoke softly. "Do you really think I am handsome?"

"Okay. On a scale from one to ten, one being ugly and ten being muy guapo, I would rate you a twenty at the least." Andrew gave him a huge smile. "What can I say?"

"Andrew. Thank you for being so kind to me. I hope you do not mind but I do feel tired. Would you mind if I went to bed?"

"Mi casa es tu casa. Remember that." He pointed toward the bedrooms. "Okay. Bedtime. See you in the morning."

"Buenas noches, mi amigo." Armando smiled as he went into the bedroom.

"Buenas noches, mi amigo." Andrew responded, going into his.

After all the lights were out and Andrew was lying quietly in bed, he yelled out. "¡Buenas noches, John Boy!"

Armando called out from the master bedroom. "What!? John Boy!?"

Andrew replied laughing. "Not to worry. You had to be there. I'll explain sometime."

CHAPTER VI

Over the next several days, they enjoyed each other's company, talking about many things. There were no walls preventing certain conversations. Nothing was taboo. Andrew noticed how intensely Armando listened when talking about virtually everything. He watched him perusing the books in the bookcase. He attributed it to the possibility Armando liked to read.

The cut on Armando's head was healing nicely but still, it would need time to completely heal and go away.

Armando entertained Andrew several times with his guitar playing. One evening as they sat in the living room and Armando had just finished playing, he looked at Andrew and smiled. "I want to hear you play something on the piano for me."

"Oh, all right. There are two pieces I've been thinking about that seem to be rather apropos here. The first one because of where we are. By the ocean. The second, knowing one day soon, you're going to have to leave and get on with your own life. We will part ways. I hope you can take my singing."

"The first one is one I'll play for you soon on the CD player. To me, the most wonderful rendition was done by the Righteous Brothers. And the way Bobby Hatfield hits that last note at the end is enough to make the hairs on your arms stand up, it's so beautiful. It's called *Ebb Tide*." Andrew started playing and sang the song but without the spectacular Bobby Hatfield ending. His rendition was significantly more reserved and traditional.

"That is a beautiful song." Armando spoke softly. "I do look forward to hearing it on the CD player, too."

"The next one was played and sung by so many people. Even Rosemary Clooney sang it. I heard that Liberace used to end all his performances with it. I like it because it makes me remember all my friends, especially those who are no longer here. He turned and glanced at the portrait on the wall. It is called *I'll Be Seeing You*."

Andrew played the opening notes of the melancholy melody then began the words. "'I'll be seeing you… in all the old familiar places… that this heart of mine embraces… all day through…'" Andrew sang with all the emotion the song evokes, closing his eyes to keep his tears from falling as images of long-lost friends passed through his mind. He also thought of Jacob. Finally, coming to the end, he was playing and singing with a significant retard. "'I'll see you in the morning sun… and when the night is new…… I'll be looking at the moon…… but I'll be seeing…… you.'" With the scale up the keyboard, getting softer with each note, there was finally the last pianissimo bass chord. Andrew held the chord until it faded away. He turned his head to the left to hide his emotions. There was a long silence as he gained his composure.

He turned to Armando and smiled. He was overwhelmed to see Armando, sitting there silent, biting his lower lip with tears streaming down his cheeks and into the dark hair of his beard.

Armando buried his head in his hands and began to sob. "Andrew. It is such a beautiful song but it is so sad. It makes me hurt. It makes me think and remember those I used to know who I miss so much. It is so sad."

Andrew came over, patted and grabbed Armando on the shoulders. He tried to be upbeat. "But isn't that a wonderful way to remember someone?" He smiled but he couldn't hide his own tears.

Armando looked up, wiping his face. He smiled. "Yes. Yes, it is." He stood up and hugged Andrew. "Thank you so much. Both of those songs are so wonderful."

"Yes. To me, it's a very powerful song. I think of all those people who mean so much and meant so much to me and how badly I miss them." Andrew wiped his own face with his hands.

Andrew walked over to the shelf of CDs and located the one of the Righteous Brothers. Within minutes, the voices of Bobby Hatfield and Bill Medley filled the room. As Bobby sang the last two words, hitting the final high note, finally fading to silence, Andrew smiled at Armando. "See what I mean? Isn't that incredible?"

Armando was excited. "How amazing. You must play it again for me sometime."

"Now. How would you like one more cup of tea before we hit the hay?"

Armando smiled and winked his right eye.

CHAPTER VII

The next morning, it was to the grocery store to get a few things. Armando loved riding in the Jeep. He liked the open air.

As they were bringing everything into the house, Andrew turned to Armando. "While I put things away and organize for dinner later on, why don't you go try out the boat and do a little sailing? I think you're well enough now. Don't forget to put on some sunscreen. And I'll come down to the beach when I get done here."

Armando flexed his eyebrows. "That sounds like a great idea. I will be careful." He headed to the cove where the boat was anchored.

Finishing putting things away, Andrew grabbed his camera then went to the beach. He could see the boat out beyond the surf. It was stationary and Armando was not in it. He became alarmed. "Holy God! He fell out of the boat!" He ran to the edge of the water.

Suddenly, he saw Armando emerge from below the water. He was holding something in his hand which he tossed in the boat then disappeared beneath the surface. "What the hell is he doing?" He stood and waited. He saw him surface but immediately went below again. Shortly, he came up again and threw something else in the boat then climbed in. He raised the sail and headed to shore. He saw Andrew and waved.

As Armando pulled the boat into the cove, Andrew yelled out. "Jesus H! You know. You're going to be the death of me. I thought you had fallen overboard… again!"

Armando tied down the sail and anchored the boat. Walking toward Andrew, he held up his catch and smiled. He had two large lobsters. "How does this look for dinner?"

Andrew raised his camera and took a picture. "Wow. I was told they were out there among the rocks but never have gone looking for them. That was going to be Jacob's job. I guess it now falls to you." Andrew grinned. "Yes. Perfect. Dinner! Thank you."

"What is that?" Armando looked at the camera.

"Thought I would take some pictures. I can put a few more around the house next to the ones of Jacob and me."

Armando chuckled. "I am sorry. I am so used to the cameras being so much bigger than the one you have."

They walked up to the house and Andrew put the creatures in the kitchen sink. He wet a kitchen towel and placed it over them. "That'll keep them happy till dinner. You know these things are twelve dollars a pound in the stores in the States."

Armando went to the master bedroom to get out of his bathing suit and dry off. He returned to the kitchen in shorts and a T-shirt.

"Well. It's almost two o'clock. What about a Whiskey Sour?" Andrew reached for two glasses from the cabinet. He rubbed a piece of lime around the rims and coated them in sugar. From the fridge, he grabbed the big jar of mixed cocktail and filled the glasses. "These should have a slice of orange but the maraschino cherry and lime wedge will have to suffice." He handed one to Armando.

"After we finish our drink, let us go walk on the beach." Armando suggested.

"I would like that. And don't forget the sunscreen! I'll bring the camera and take some more pictures."

They had been on the beach for almost two hours when they stopped just looking out at the water. Armando pointed at a rock outcropping in the sand. "Let us go sit down."

The formation was not conducive to sitting but it did allow Andrew to put the bottle of sunscreen down. They leaned back against the rock, looking out at the surf. He walked out about ten feet, turned. "Okay. Smile!"

"Click". The camera sounded.

"Now. Just one more but you have to come out here." Armando came to the spot where Andrew was standing. "Just a minute. I have to get it ready." He ran over to the rock, placed the camera on it, pointing in Armando's direction. He fiddled with it for a few seconds then turned and ran toward Armando. He stood by him and then called out. "Now! Smile and don't move."

"Click." The camera sounded.

"Don't move. I'll take one more just to make sure. It's the last one on the roll." Andrew ran to the camera again, set it then ran back to Armando who put his arm around Andrew's shoulder. "Smile."

"Click." Another picture was taken.

They walked back to the rock and leaned against it, watching the surf roll in.

"Andrew. How do I ever thank you for the last week? You have been so kind. I cannot tell you how relaxing it has been for me. I would have never done this alone. I would never have considered it. You have shown me a wonderful time. I am enjoying it so much." He paused for a moment and a worried expression came to his face. "There is something I need to tell you. I need to explain. I am not quite sure how to begin. I do not even understand it myself. It is so very strange and will sound crazy."

Andrew became concerned. "I hope it's not to tell me you have to go soon. I have truly enjoyed you being here with me. I enjoy your company. I like you. You have a fantastic personality. You're considerate and kind. Please, don't tell me you have to leave. You know I will miss you."

Armando bent his head down and shook it before responding. "Interesting you should say that because it does have to do with my possible departure. I swear it is so insane. But maybe I should try and figure it out myself before we talk about it. Yes. I will do that."

"Okay. If you say so. But let me know when you want to talk. I can see it on your face that whatever it is really is of great concern to you."

"Thank you so much. I will. It may take a while for me to put the puzzle together. But, if I should go away, will you play *I'll Be Seeing You* and remember me?" Armando looked intently at Andrew.

Andrew looked up at Armando and spoke softly. "Yes. I will play it and I will miss you. I will miss you very much." He looked out to sea. "This last week has been unbelievable for me as well. I feel comfortable with you. I feel free. I've not felt this way since..." He paused in his memory.

"Andrew. I understand. And I thank you for putting me in such incredible company. I feel the same way. Our friendship has grown quickly but I feel it is genuine. We have shared time and conversation that has been very helpful and rewarding to me. I could never have come to this point without your help, letting me see things through different eyes and understanding. I know we will be friends forever. But no. I am not leaving. At least I do not think I am. It is so much more. Something very strange. But not to worry. I will figure it out and then we will talk."

"That makes me feel better. I want you to stay here as long as you like. When it is time you must go, I will understand. You may have money but I also realize you have obligations and business to take care of just as I do. I cannot stay here forever, either. Well. Not until I retire. That doesn't mean we can't stay in touch and share time together with visits. Remember. Wherever I am, my door will always be open to you."

"I have never met anyone like you. You are like an open book. So many I come in contact with are so devious and conniving. I think they see money before the man."

Andrew agreed. "I have never understood it. Money cannot buy you happiness. If you have no connection to the one you are with, all the money in the world won't fix it. As for looks, let me tell you. I have met some very good-looking people who I knew would never make good friends, much less anything more, because they had zero personality. No qualities that would make them a good person. And looks fade."

He paused for a moment. "I remember Jacob asking me one day. He asked if I would still love and care for him if he got burned and disfigured in a fire." Andrew paused again and shook his head. "Geez. How prophetic his words were. It never hit me till now. Wow!"

He was silent for a moment before continuing where he'd left off. He turned to Armando and with his right index finger, pointed to the spot between his eyes. "I pointed right at his face, just like I'm doing to you and told him, it was the man behind his eyes I loved. His good looks were just icing on the cake." He took his finger away.

"There's a wonderful old movie that expresses it so well. Robert Young and Dorothy McGuire. 'The Enchanted Cottage.' It's a great tearjerker. Mildred Natwick has the most incredible lines. She's the elderly lady who has owned the cottage since her honeymoon and whose husband died at sea when they were young. She's explaining the secret of the cottage. I can't remember the exact words she speaks but she says if her husband ever came walking in the door, she would see him tall, handsome and strong and he would look at her and see her beautiful and desirable, just as they did when they were together. Needless to say, after she says her poignant lines, I am bawling like all get out. We need to watch that movie. Maybe tonight before we go to sleep."

"I like the premise of it already. Maybe someone will love me like that one day. I would hope to meet such a person." Armando turned to Andrew. "I just wanted you to know how much I am enjoying this time with you. It is very special to me."

"Well, thank you. I think it's time for dinner. Let's head back to the house." He gave Armando a soft punch to his shoulder. "We'll watch that movie after dinner."

Andrew steamed up the lobsters along with some broccoli in cheese sauce. A big salad and a chilled white wine rounded it out. Afterward, Andrew cleared the dishes and poured two glasses of iced tea for them. They went to the living room and got comfortable to watch the movie. When it was over, neither could hide the emotions it had brought out.

Andrew giggled as he wiped his face of the tears. "I'm sorry. I can't help it. These movies just take me over the top. I think they're so wonderful. I wish they made them like that today instead of all those blow-up everything and all action kind. The ones today rarely have any social commentary or carry any major human connection. Not like all those old movies."

"I have rarely seen anything that has had such an impact on me emotionally like that movie did. There have been books but watching it acted out is so different from reading a book." Armando agreed.

Andrew continued. "Jane Austen. She's so great. I have her books, Pride and Prejudice and Persuasion as movies on DVDs. We'll have to watch them, too."

Armando nodded. "Thank you so much, again. All this is so amazing to me."

"I'm so glad I found you out there. I know you went through trauma to get here but I'm glad you did." He stood up and stretched his arms in the air. "Guess it's time to turn in. See you tomorrow. Buenas noches."

"Buenas noches." Armando headed to the master bedroom.

Andrew went to his room, removed his clothes, turned off the light and got in bed. He could hear the pounding surf outside which was always calming to him. The night was warm, so he lay on top of the sheets.

As his eyes became accustomed to the dimness of the night, he heard his door open and Armando came in, standing in the dark at the foot of his bed. He whispered. "Armando. Is everything all right? Do you need something?"

"Andrew." He spoke softly. "May I. May I be with you tonight?"

Andrew was totally taken aback. He was so surprised. "Are you sure?"

"Yes. I want to be near you. Are you angry with me?"

"No. No. I just wanted to make sure. If it is what you want. Come. Get in bed. I would like you to be near me. I would like it very much."

Armando climbed in, lying next to Andrew, pulling him close. "Thank you, mi amigo." He whispered.

In no time, the sound of the surf had them both asleep.

CHAPTER VIII

Andrew awoke, lying next to Armando who was fast asleep. He couldn't believe what had happened. True. He had begun to feel a connection with him but did not realize it had poured over into the physical. He couldn't deny it. There was a comfort being with him. It felt so similar, so relaxed. Much like the way it was when with Jacob. He smiled. But it was time to get up and start breakfast. He wouldn't disturb Armando.

Breakfast was well on its way in preparation when Armando came around the corner. He looked at Andrew with a guilty expression. "Andrew. Please, forgive me. I had no right."

"Don't be silly. It was nice. I've not had that since Jacob died and it was nice to have someone there again. Someone nice, kind and considerate. And to be honest..." He looked directly at Armando. "I don't mind if it continues. And I hope it does. There. I said it."

Armando gave a big smile and winked his right eye. "For me, also. It was nice to have someone next to me. I have never been able to have that before. I was not sure I should but from our conversations, I thought I could take the chance. I was so afraid you might think I was trying to move in on the feelings you have for Jacob."

He looked right at Armando. "Just because you care for one person does not mean you can't care for another. You said it yourself. The cup of caring and love is never empty. It's always full. There's always enough to share with many. It may be different but it doesn't diminish what is given to another. Exactly like you said. Remember that."

"I cannot explain it but I feel so comfortable and free with you. And I wanted to be near you. Thank you for letting me be with you."

"I'm glad you feel free and comfortable with me. It makes me feel good to know that. And if you like, I'll come stay with you in my… your bedroom." Andrew grinned. "Our bedroom." He chuckled and turned to the stove. "Now. Are you ready for something to eat? Then, we can go down to the beach. You should go sailing today. I know you love it."

"Thank you, Andrew. We can sleep together in… our bedroom." He grinned and winked his right eye. "And as for sailing, come with me? I'll not let you fall overboard."

Andrew looked back at Armando and they started to laugh, growing louder and louder. "Okay. Here's your coffee. Omelets in a few minutes."

After breakfast, they went to the beach and pushed off the boat. Armando raised the sail and they were off. He maneuvered the boat through the rock formations and out to open water. They were out for several hours.

Andrew was not one for much sailing but with Armando at the helm, it was a pleasant and invigorating experience. He'd asked him not to go out of the sight of land since he had a terrible phobia about it. He couldn't explain why but not being able to see the land could give him a major panic attack. It was one reason he could never get himself to take a cruise. Buying the boat was for Jacob but it was also for another reason. He thought it might help him get over his fear if he took it out now and then.

It was mid-afternoon when they pulled back into the little cove. Armando tied down the sail and anchored the boat. They headed to the house.

"Let's make a trip into town before I start dinner. I want to drop off my roll of film, so they can print the pictures. They are so nice there. They do professional photography. You know. Weddings and special events. I got to know them when I came down here last year. I was looking for a good photographer just in case I might need one for some party or event I might throw here at the house. Hey! Business! You never know. And it's always good to be prepared. Have to tell you. It's getting more and more difficult to find a place to do it with all this digital stuff nowadays. Cameras, using actual film, are becoming extinct."

Pulling up to the small business, they got out and went inside.

"¡Hola, Hector y María! ¿Cómo estás?" Andrew smiled, seeing the owners as he and Armando entered.

Armando quickly jumped in. "Your Spanish really needs work. It should be están when you are talking to more than one person." He gave a big Cheshire Cat grin.

This made everyone laugh.

Andrew continued. "I brought a roll of film in, so you can make some prints of my photos. I would like two copies of each picture."

"¡Señor Andrew! ¡Hola! We can do that for you. How have you been? We have not seen you in so long." María smiled.

"Work. You know. I only get to come down here once a year in February. I won't be here permanently till I'm old enough to retire."

"Sí. I understand. But where is Señor Jacob? Is he not with you this trip?" She had a questioning look on her face.

Andrew bent his head down and spoke in a quiet voice. "Oh, María. Jacob died last May. He died fighting a fire."

"¡Oh, Señor Andrew! I am so sorry! I am so sorry!" She crossed herself. "I could tell he was a fine man. Rest his soul." She embraced Andrew.

Hector, too, spoke up. "Sí. I am so sorry."

María then looked at Armando.

"Oh, María. This is my friend, Armando. He lives in Acapulco."

"¡Hola, Señor Armando! Bienvenido." Her face cringed as she looked up at his forehead. "Señor Armando. What happened to your head? It has scarred your very handsome face."

"Gracias, Señora." Armando slightly bowed his head and smiled. "I had an accident in the ocean. I hit my head on a rock."

"Well. I hope it heals all right. It would be a shame to mar such a face. Señor Armando. Are you a model?" María gave a big smile.

Armando looked at Andrew.

Andrew began to chuckle. "No, María. But he sure could be one, couldn't he?"

"Well. If he should ever need any professional pictures done, we would be happy to do them."

"What a great idea!" Andrew clapped his hands together. He turned to Armando. "Would you mind if Hector did some nice professional pictures of you? I know they would be wonderful."

Armando flexed his eyebrows. "Why not."

Andrew turned to Hector. "Do you think you would have some time tomorrow? I could bring him in and you could do a few shots." He paused for a moment. "Oh. But they might not be done in time. Armando may have to leave when I do near the end of the month."

Hector turned to Andrew. "Señor Andrew. Come in tomorrow, so I can take the pictures. For you, we can have them ready in two days. And not to worry about that thing on your head. I can airbrush it out. You can pick up the pictures from your camera, too."

"Perfect! That would be terrific! See you tomorrow. How about around nine tomorrow morning?" Andrew and Armando started to head out of the shop.

"That would be great. Take care. And again. I am so sorry about Señor Jacob. Que tenga un buen día. Hasta mañana." María waved.

"Igualmente, María. Gracias. Mañana." Andrew called back.

After dinner, they watched another movie from Andrew's extensive collection. 'Wuthering Heights' with Laurence Olivier and Merle Oberon filled the screen.

As the movie ended, Armando spoke. "What an intense love they had for one another. I can see a love like that lasting beyond death. I wonder if someone could ever love me with such intensity?" He took a drink of his iced tea.

"With the kind of man I see in you already, I would think so. And I believe you, too, could love someone like that. Maybe tomorrow night we'll watch 'Jane Eyre' with Joan Fontaine and Orson Wells. I love the Brontë sisters." He smiled. "Okay. It's getting late. I guess we should call it a night." Andrew got up and reached down, grabbing Armando's hand. "Let's go hit the hay."

Armando looked up at Andrew and flexed his eyebrows.

The next day, Andrew made up the bed in the third bedroom again since he and Armando were now sharing the same bed in the master bedroom. Then, they got ready to go into Zihuatanejo for Armando's photoshoot. It was also time for a little sightseeing and a stop at the fish market.

As Hector was posing Armando and taking a few pictures, María was talking to Andrew and saying how handsome Armando was. "Andrew. Seriously. With his looks, he could be a high-paid model."

"María. Trust me. Money doesn't seem to be a problem for him."

"How did you meet him?"

Andrew just shook his head. "I'll tell you that story one of these days. I can tell you this. When you hear it, I don't think you'll believe me." He called out to Hector. "Hector. Make sure you make two sets."

Armando spoke up. "Hector. Could you make one set for me just as I am? With my cut still on my head? If you would not mind?"

"Certainly. I will make three sets and one will have your cut as it is right now. But why?" Hector looked puzzled.

Armando smiled. "I have my reason."

Session over, Hector indicated they could come by and pick everything up in two days. Expressing thanks, they were out the door and off to the airport in Zihuatanejo to check and confirm Andrew's tickets back to Atlanta right after the first of March. While there, they got to see one of the airlines load passengers and take off.

Armando couldn't take his eyes off the plane, watching it leave the ground and fly through the air. "It is amazing how something made of metal and holding all those people can actually get off the ground and fly through the air."

They watched the aircraft disappear into the clouds.

Andrew responded. "I know what you mean. It has always astounded me, too, but I know it has to do with the wings creating lift. I feel the same way about big ships made of metal and how they stay afloat. Again, I know it has to do with buoyancy and water displacement. Yeah. But still." He then changed the subject. "Thought we could see some of the shopping arcades, see one of the churches and check out the fish market to see what we can get for dinner. I brought the cooler in case we saw something really good there."

Armando agreed. "That sounds like fun."

There were several shops where they stopped. Andrew bought them each a big straw hat to keep off the sun. Next, they went to the fish market on the Bay of Zihuatanejo. Andrew loved the fish market. The prices were extremely reasonable and the fish had just come off the boats of the local fishermen. True, the best time is very early in the morning as that's when they first get in from the sea. When you come later, you have to take what is left. But the choices were still very good.

Armando spotted some beautiful snapper. "I think I see dinner." He pointed at one of the fish displayed on the ice.

"Snapper it is!" Andrew replied.

Just then, Andrew looked out into the bay. "Oh! Look! One of the cruise ships is in. They come down the coast from California with tourists."

Armando just stared out at the ship anchored in the bay. He smiled and spoke softly. "Yes. Yes, I see."

Andrew turned and pointed. "The law firm where I went to buy the lot here is right over in that direction. Yep. The Vargas Law Firm. Very nice folks work there."

On the way back, they stopped at the church in Zihuatanejo. They parked and went in.

Armando went to the front and genuflected before kneeling in front of the main altar. Andrew joined him. Shortly, Armando got up and went to the candles, lighting one. He turned to Andrew. "It is to thank God for letting me meet you. I now know He sees no wrong in our friendship."

"I couldn't agree with you more. Thank you, Armando."

After looking around at the church, they got back in the Jeep and were headed home. When they arrived, Armando grabbed the cooler. Andrew got the hats. They headed inside.

"How about a glass of iced tea? I'll fix us a little something to munch on to hold us till dinner." He pulled out some chips and the queso dip he'd made in advance from the fridge and stuck it in the microwave. "Let me check my email. I haven't done it since you got here. Everyone will think I'm dead. I hope there's internet. It's not the greatest here." He went to the main bedroom and got his computer, placing it on the dining table. "I need to get your email address before you leave, so I can connect with you on your computer. Remind me."

"I do not have an email address."

"You have to be kidding me. Don't tell me you're one of those last holdouts who STILL writes letters and actually mails them? And now, you'll also tell me you have no cell phone." He looked, rolled his eyes and shook his head. "I guess I shouldn't say anything. My cell phone is the first one I've owned. I hated that I had to get one but it became almost impossible not to have one. So, I shouldn't be surprised someone else would be doing just what I did. Okay, so I'll need your address in Acapulco. We can write letters." He snickered.

"Yes. We can write letters." Armando smiled then sat down at the dining table.

Andrew continued. "You must have the same love-hate relationship with computers and technology that I do. They can be such a pain but they can be so helpful, too, especially if you need to find something out about a subject. I think all the information of the world is accessible on computers. If you ever want to use mine, let me know. I'll get you on to whatever you want. As I said, the internet here is a bit sketchy. It's the law firm in Zihuatanejo which oversees the whole parcel, who installed the tower here back in two thousand and three and pays for the service. I told them I had no problem paying a fee but they were totally insistent they'd take care of it. Hey. I'm not complaining."

Andrew turned on the computer. "Okay. Let me see." He waited as the laptop powered up. He checked the internet. "Yes! We have internet!" He yelled out.

"I should watch you and see. That way I will not mess anything up." Armando got up and stood behind Andrew, watching as he went in and started perusing his emails.

"I know what you mean. Seems every damn computer is different. Let me show you how I found a great recipe the other day." He backed out to the main page. "Just went up here to this space here, typed in the name then clicked on the 'search' block. Here, let me show you."

Armando watched diligently as Andrew moved the mouse and clicked the information bar at the top of the screen. "Okay. What do you want to know more about?"

"How about those airplanes we saw today?"

Andrew typed in the block then clicked on the blue box with the magnifying glass in it. "See? Anything. And look at all the selections you have about the damn things. Click on any one of them and you can find out all about them. From the Wright brothers, all the way up to present time. Actually, there may even be stuff about Da Vinci and his thinking, regarding flight."

"Really? Anything?"

"Anything. If it's out there, it can be found on the computer. From dinosaurs, the universe, to little-known historical facts. Here. I'll show you one more." He typed 'Titanic' in the search block.

"Titanic?" Armando questioned.

"Yes. All that is possibly available about it from its construction to its sinking in April of nineteen twelve."

"Really? Its sinking as well?"

"Greatest ocean liner disaster in history. And that's just one historic event you can find using a computer. I think it truly is amazing. Play with it for a while. And you know. I hate to say it but I think they are going to replace books eventually. Computers make it too easy."

Andrew let Armando use the computer as he got the iced tea and hot queso, placing them on the table. "Let me get the chips."

Armando continued to amuse himself at the computer while Andrew started dinner. Periodically, he would ask Andrew to get him back to a place after hitting the wrong key or clicking the wrong box but he was enjoying it. "Would you mind if I used it once in a while? I am so amazed at what you can find in here."

"Of course. You can use it anytime. Just let me know and I'll get it out for you. Tell you what, I'll leave it here on the table and you can use it whenever you like. I'll plug it in, so the battery doesn't run down."

"I would like that." Armando was amazed. He had found a new toy and would get on it quite frequently when Andrew was busy with other things.

Andrew started the grill and placed a piece of screen on it. He always used it when grilling small things, preventing them from falling through the regular grill rungs. It was perfect to cook the fish and not have it flake and fall into the coals. He thought it so dumb. Many use aluminum foil on their grill. There was no way the grilling flavor could penetrate the foil and get to the food. It might as well have been cooked in the oven or on top of the stove. He did understand if it was summer and the weather hot. It would prevent getting the kitchen and the house heated up. Now, that did make sense.

Armando sat across from Andrew. "I swear. You are such a good cook. I cannot believe it. I wish I had someone like you cooking in my kitchens."

"You know, my father says I cook so well I'd make someone a great wife."

They looked at one another and burst out laughing.

Armando nodded his head. "Well. It is true."

With dinner over, they went and sat in the living room. Andrew went to get them more tea. When he got back, he looked at Armando and smiled. Suddenly, he saw the distress on Armando's face. Tears were running down his cheeks. He set the glasses of tea down and grabbed Armando's shoulder. "Armando. What's wrong? What has happened?"

"Oh, Andrew. I am SO afraid. I have never been so free. So happy. I have never enjoyed being with someone before like this. I am so afraid something is going to happen and it will end. It is the puzzle I am trying to figure out and understand. It is making me crazy." He shivered as if hit with a chill. "I like you. I am having fun for the first time in my life. I do not want it to end. I do not want our friendship to end. I am afraid if it does, I will never get it back again." He stood up and hugged Andrew.

"It's all right. We're friends and nothing can change that. Our friendship will never end. Even if we part as we must to continue our obligations and duties. Nothing will change for us. We can stay in touch and even visit one another. I'd like that. I've always told you. You're always welcome to visit me whenever you like. Armando, you're very special. That will never change."

They sat down. Armando looked hauntingly at Andrew. "But there is something I need to tell you. I have had it on my mind almost as long as I have been here. I am so afraid I will get pulled back. I do not want to leave."

"Armando, I don't want you to leave but soon we both will have to get back to our obligations. Do not worry. Our friendship is solid. Don't concern yourself. You and I will stay in touch while our relationship grows."

Armando shook his head. "What you say is wonderful but the issue is so very strange and seems impossible. I am afraid something will happen to take me away from you."

"You will soon have to get to San Francisco and help your brother. I will have to get back to Atlanta and do my catering. That doesn't matter. We will still continue what we are building with our relationship regardless of where we are."

Armando nodded. "It is so unbelievable and there really is nothing I can do except to accept it all and hope for the best. I will continue to work on it and see if there is a solution. If I find one, I will talk with you about it."

Andrew agreed. "That sounds good. Now, let's finish our tea and I'll fix us a Gin and Tonic and we can go take a walk on the beach?"

"Yes. I would like that." Armando smiled and seemed to cheer up.

They took a long walk on the beach. Finally, they leaned against the rock they had the other day. The moon was up. It made the night brighter than normal.

Armando sang softly, as he looked up. "'I'll… I'll be looking at the moon…. but I'll be seeing…. you.'" He paused for a moment. "Andrew. Every time I look at the moon, I will be thinking about you." He looked at Andrew and smiled.

"That was so nice to say. You, too, will be in my heart and my thoughts." Andrew smiled back and paused for a moment. "I was thinking. I should do a painting. Yeah. A sunset. One like we saw the other day. I think I can capture the beauty on canvas. Painting the ocean is a bitch, though. But that's okay. I just might have to do one."

"From the other paintings you have done, hanging in the house, I do not think you will have any problem." Armando was reassuring.

The night was clear, the moon shone brightly and the stars were sparkling in the sky when they went back to the house. They went to the living room and started the DVD of 'Jane Eyre'. Several times during the movie, Andrew hit the pause button, so he could refresh their drinks. He knew the right places since he had seen the movie numerous times. He fixed more queso dip, too.

"See." Andrew looked at Armando when the movie ended and smiled. "Time and distance did not keep them apart. Even with all the turmoil and adversity, they got back together."

Armando smiled back. He turned to the doorway. "It is starting to rain."

"Where did that come from? It's really strange as this is not the rainy season. The night was so clear earlier. We might need a blanket if it gets too chilly."

Armando winked his right eye. "I will keep you warm." He had a huge Cheshire Cat grin on his face.

Andrew just smiled. "No comment."

They both chuckled.

The rain did not last long that night. Just enough to wash the slight dust off everything. Morning arrived with bright sunlight and a cool breeze. After a quick breakfast, Armando thought he would go sailing and see if he could catch more lobsters. "When I come back, I might play on the computer some more if it is all right?"

"Not a problem. Just be careful out there!" Andrew yelled as Armando started down to the beach.

It was the perfect time to start something he'd been thinking about for several days. Andrew went into the third bedroom and set his easel up and got out his paints. There already were numerous stretched canvases in the closet along with many frames. Rummaging through them, he found a twenty-four by thirty inch canvas as well as an appropriate frame. They would be superb for his project. He quickly placed paint on his palette and poured the turpentine into a glass jar. Next, his brushes went into the jar to get them ready.

Several strokes of a pencil and he had the placement of the subject on the white surface. With a little more detail, he knew he was ready for the paint. He began.

After a few hours, the background colors and base colors were in place. He was amazed at how quickly it was happening. It was like some great artist from the past was guiding his brushes. He looked at the clock and knew he had to stop. Armando would be coming home soon. After all, it was going on two o'clock. He covered the canvas with a cloth, shut the bedroom door and headed out to the beach.

Looking out to sea, he could see Armando far out. He seemed to be having a wonderful time with the boat racing through the water. Andrew smiled. He couldn't believe how happy he was. He couldn't deny it. Armando coming into his life was an amazing thing. He felt alive again. He felt caring from another person. He felt a friendship he hadn't known since Jacob. Yes. He appreciated his solitude but he'd missed the times he'd shared with Jacob. And now, he was feeling those old feelings again. He liked it.

He watched Armando turn the boat and head toward shore. Right through the rocks, it was eventually in the cove.

Andrew yelled out. "Did you have a good time?"

Armando yelled. "I had a wonderful time. You should have come with me."

"I was busy. Next time."

Armando approached Andrew. "What is this on your face?" He took his finger and wiped the spot. "It is paint. You have started a painting. How wonderful. Can I see it?"

"No. Not until it's done." Andrew smiled.

"Okay. I can wait." Armando put his arm around Andrew's back, as they walked to the house. "I did not get any lobsters. I hope you do not mind."

"Hey. So, the lobsters live to be caught another day."

This comment made them both chuckle.

"So, what are you painting?"

"Remember that sunset we saw? Well."

"When will it be done?"

"Actually, it may be finished sooner than I thought. The paint just flew onto the canvas and all in the right places. I'm quite pleased so far. Maybe a week. But I'll really have to work at it."

"Great. I know it is going to be spectacular." Armando gave Andrew a huge smile.

"How about a Whiskey Sour while I get dinner started?"

"I would like that."

As Andrew started browning the ground beef and cutting up all the fixings for spaghetti sauce, Armando sat at the dining table. He took a sip of his cocktail. "I know I have said it before but I am so happy and having a terrific time. Yes, it may sound silly but I am so afraid someone is going to pinch me and I will wake up and it will have all been a dream. What can I say?"

"There are some things we have no control over. No one knows tomorrow. So, just enjoy today. 'Carpe diem' and all that. I, too, have enjoyed what we are sharing together. But I'm taking it one step at a time. There used to be a time I looked forward to my vacations so much, I virtually couldn't enjoy them for fear they would end too fast. And you know what? They did. I finally learned to know they were coming and to appreciate each and every day I had to the fullest while on vacation. I'm doing this now with you. I'm taking the pleasure of every moment, every day with you. Yes. Soon, we'll go our separate ways but I don't think about that. I think about right now. You, sitting there at the table, having your drink, talking with me and me, here, fixing spaghetti. I'm loving every moment. I couldn't be happier."

Armando agreed. "You are right. I am so afraid of it ending, I am not focusing and enjoying the present and the happiness I am feeling because of it. I must stop my obsessing." He took another sip. "Spaghetti. I love spaghetti. Are you sure you do not need me to do anything?"

"Too many cooks spoil the broth. But you can set the table and open a red wine, so it can breathe a bit before we eat."

After dinner, Andrew put on a few CDs and turned the sound up, so they could hear it while sitting out on the terrace. After a few moments of quiet, Andrew sipped his wine and spoke. "I know all I said earlier and God knows I don't want you to leave but are you sure you don't need to contact your brother in San Francisco? I know they must be frantic, knowing you were blown off the ship." He gave a loud gasp. "Oh, my God! I'll bet they've already had your funeral! Oh, my God!"

Armando started to laugh and clap his hands. "I bet you are right. Is it not going to be funny when I show up? Alive? I can only imagine the look on his face." He laughed even louder. "But actually, it will be good for him to get things started on his own. He has everything I sent on the ship to get everything going. When I show up later and pick him up off the floor, I can tell him how pleased I am he did it all by himself. It will show him he is capable of doing things and making decisions on his own."

"All right. I just was thinking. But if you say so."

"Everything will be fine. He really does not need me. And I sure need this." He raised his glass toward Andrew.

"So do I." Andrew raised his glass.

They just sat, taking in the soft breeze. Soon, Armando spoke up. "I am tired. I think it is time for me to go to bed."

"I will come in shortly. I want to see if I might throw a bit more paint at that canvas."

"Okay. Later." Armando went to the master bedroom where they both were now sleeping.

Andrew went into the third bedroom, took the cloth off the canvas and sat down. Before he realized it, almost two hours had passed. But the time spent was well worth it. Again, he had surprised himself with the amount of progress taking place on the canvas. Shape and form, the colors, all were coming together unbelievably better than expected. He had to sleep. He stuck the brushes in the jar of turpentine, covered the canvas and headed to bed.

He didn't turn on the light, so not to wake Armando. Feeling his way to the side of the bed, he removed his clothes. Slowly and quietly, he climbed in and put his head on the pillow. Immediately, Armando's arm came over him and around his body, pulling him close. A quiet voice came from the dark. "How is the sunset coming along?"

"Armando, I'm sorry I woke you. I had no idea I was going to be in there so long."

"Do not be silly. I was waiting for you. I know you have things to do and I cannot interrupt what you do. I am only a guest here with you."

"Listen to me. You are more than any guest. Geez. I don't normally sleep with my guests."

Laughter filled the darkness for a minute or two. Then, there was only the sound of the surf hitting the beach.

CHAPTER IX

They got in the Jeep and headed in to see Hector and María. The photos were ready.

Hector opened the folder and spread the professional shots over the counter.

Andrew drew a breath. "Hector. These are wonderful. You do such excellent work. An artist you are with your camera. Even the ones of Armando with the cut on his forehead. Wow!"

"Gracias, Señor Andrew. But it is easy when you have such a man as Armando." Hector nodded.

Armando smiled. "Gracias, Hector."

María brought the pictures from Andrew's camera and spread them on the counter.

"Look at you!" Andrew picked up the picture of Armando, holding up the two lobsters and began to snicker.

Armando took the picture and giggled.

"María, do you have some frames I can get for the pictures? I want to put them up when I get home."

"Certainly. Since the pictures are standard size, any of these would be satisfactory."

"Perfect." Andrew started looking through the selection of frames and picked out several. "Thank you so much. I do appreciate you doing them so fast. Guess I won't see you all until next February. Take care and be safe." Andrew hugged María and shook Hector's hand.

"Yes. Thank you so much. The pictures are excellent." Armando hugged María and shook Hector's hand.

"Señor Andrew. I will light a candle and say a prayer for Señor Jacob." María gave a caring smile.

"Gracias, María. Gracias. And I'll see you next February. ¡Adiós!" Andrew smiled, turned and they left the shop.

Getting home, Andrew separated the pictures. He gave Armando a complete set of all the pictures as well as the set with the cut on his head. He looked at the ones taken on the beach. "Now, you have something to put in your wallet. I know the professional ones won't fit. You'll have to fold them."

Armando nodded. "You are right." He reached into his back pocket and pulled out his empty wallet. Arranging the pictures, he stuck them in one of the pockets. "Yes, I will have to fold them but they are so wonderful. I have never had anything like it before."

"They are yours. I had them made for you. And we can always have duplicates made. Hector has the negatives."

"I do not want to put the pictures in my wallet just to have something in it. I want them there, so you will always be close to me. Wherever I may be, you will be also."

Andrew began to put the pictures in the frames, placing them around the living room. He took one of the pictures of both Armando and himself and placed it on the dresser in the bedroom next to the one of Jacob and himself.

Armando watched and his heart warmed at the gesture, seeing his presence next to ones of Jacob. He had to bite his lip to prevent from tearing up.

Over the next several days, they stayed at the house or the beach. Armando went sailing several times, occasionally bringing back lobsters for dinner. Andrew was ecstatic, knowing how much they cost per pound in Atlanta. Of course, they were the Spiny lobsters and not the typical Maine ones but it didn't matter. They tasted great.

During the times Armando was out, he had time to work on the painting. The quick and excellent progress he had made with it was extremely pleasing to him. He was sure he could get it done in just a few days.

The days with Armando were like a gift. Andrew was so happy and felt so alive. He also came to realize Armando was becoming more than a friend. He couldn't say anything as he had known him for such a short period of time. But his relationship with Jacob gave him the experience to sort out what he liked and wanted in a major relationship. And he was beginning to have those feelings again.

Armando enjoyed his time on the ocean. It gave him time to think, weigh and balance things in his head. He'd never had this kind of happiness ever before in his life. Never had there been feelings for someone like those he had for Andrew. He'd close his eyes and thank God for the happiness he was experiencing. But he was not sure how to handle the dilemma he was in and so afraid something was going to bring it all tumbling down. Then, he thought of what Andrew had told him. Not to worry about things he had no control over and not to worry but live for the day. That made him smile.

He also recalled the story of how Andrew obtained the lot where the house stood. He, being a banker and knowing the potential value of real estate, it seemed so very strange such a large parcel should remain intact for so long. And why was it that Andrew was the only one able to purchase the lot at such a low price? It was all very odd.

After securing the boat, he headed to the house, only to meet Andrew coming out with drinks. He saw Andrew hold one up in the air. "Thank you so much. You seem to know what I want before I do." He yelled out.

"I just had a feeling you could use one. I saw you returning about fifteen minutes ago."

"Did you get more done on your painting?"

"Yes. It's just happening so fast and so well. It's rather scary."

"When do I get to see it?"

"I think in about two days. I hope you'll like it as much as I do so far."

"I cannot imagine you doing an ugly painting."

"Oh. One day, I should show you my very first one. I think I was about fifteen when I did it. I have it only to remind myself as to how far I have come." He could see the painting in his mind.

"It could not be that bad." Armando had a curious expression on his face.

"Oh. Trust me. It is. But I have improved a lot over the years." His face displayed a huge grin. "Okay. Change of subject. How about hamburgers tonight?"

"Andrew. I do not care what you fix. Everything you serve me is delicious and wonderful."

"Yeah. I'll bet you tell that to all your cooks."

They broke out laughing.

Two days later, Andrew told Armando to go sailing and catch some lobsters. "Take a few hours. Don't come back until mid-afternoon."

"And what is happening here?" Armando looked puzzled.

"I should have something to show you before I fix dinner."

Armando realized he was referring to the painting. He gave a huge grin. "Lobsters it is for dinner! See you this afternoon." He ran out of the house and down the beach like some enthusiastic child.

Andrew went in and took the cover off the canvas. He stared at it intensely. He had actually finished it the night before. He just needed to look at it and see if there were any finishing touches he wanted to make.

He poured himself a mug of coffee then came in and sat in front of the painting. After several minutes, he got up and grabbed the frame he'd picked out that first day. He placed the painting in the frame. It couldn't have been more perfect. He smiled and a tear ran down his face. He was so pleased with his accomplishment. He took the painting out into the living room, got out the drill, hammer and anchor bolts. One doesn't just drive a nail into the masonry walls here in Mexico.

After about thirty minutes, the painting was hanging right next to the portrait of Jacob. It was the same size. Andrew wanted it that way. He stood back and looked at it. He was very pleased and couldn't believe how good it was. The colors and highlights almost made it real. Being the same size as Jacob's portrait, it would look wonderful as its companion. He went back to the bedroom and got the cloth. Taking it to the living room, he covered the painting. It was ready to be seen.

"Time for another mug of coffee."

It was just about an hour later when he heard Armando's voice coming from the beach. "I caught two really big ones this time."

Andrew went to the terrace to see him coming up from the beach, holding two very large lobsters up in the air. "You're back so soon. It's not even noon yet."

"Well. I got out there and before I knew it, I had both of them." He looked at the two creatures. "Andrew. I could not wait. I know you are almost done with the painting but I wanted to see it. I will wait until it is done. But I wanted to wait here with you. I can help you hang it."

"Okay. Take the lobsters in and put them in the sink. Then, go get out of your bathing suit and dry off. I'll fix you a mug of coffee and cover the lobsters."

Shortly, Armando returned to the kitchen and picked up the mug of coffee Andrew had poured for him. He turned and saw Andrew sitting in the living room.

"Come, sit down." Andrew smiled up at Armando.

Sitting next to Andrew, he looked up and saw the cloth-covered rectangle hanging on the wall. "The sunset. You HAVE finished it. I cannot wait to see it. I know it is beautiful. I will bet it is prettier than the one we saw not long ago." Armando's face was filled with excitement.

Andrew stood up and walked over to the wall and took hold of the cloth. "Are you ready?"

"Ready!" Armando looked intensely at the wall with a big smile on his face.

Andrew bent his head down. "I hope you don't mind but I told you a lie. I didn't do a sunset. I did something much more important. Please, don't be angry with me. I hope you will forgive me." Andrew carefully started removing the cloth slowly, so not to smear the wet paint. "Now, it isn't dry yet. It's going to take almost a month before it is. Now. Tell me what you think." Andrew took the cloth completely away, revealing the painting. He turned, looking at Armando.

Armando's smiling happy face slowly turned to a stunned expression. He stood up quickly, bent his head down, burying his face in his hands, sobbing uncontrollably. "Andrew. Oh, Andrew. What can I say?"

"Do you like it?" Andrew spoke softly.

"Do I like it? And you hung it there." He started sobbing again. As he wiped his eyes, trying to stop the tears, Andrew walked over to him and they both looked at the painting. "I thought you were painting a beautiful sunset. But... it is me. You painted me." Armando couldn't stop sobbing. "It is incredible. A portrait of me. And you have it hanging right next to the one of Jacob. What an honor."

"I had to do it. I felt compelled to paint you. And it went so wonderfully well. I cannot lie, though. The pictures Hector took were very helpful, too. What can I say? I'm glad you like it. It's the face of a truly handsome man."

"A truly handsome man?"

"Yes. A truly handsome man is not only handsome on the outside but he's also handsome on the inside." He smiled. "And it belongs next to the one of Jacob who was also a truly handsome man."

Armando gathered himself and hugged Andrew tightly. "Thank you. Thank you, my friend. What a wonderful thing to do for someone. You are so kind. And all I brought you were two lobsters."

"Armando. You brought me two lobsters and a wonderful man from the sea. A man who has made me happy and content. A man who has shown me friendship and caring. I've done something inanimate. You've given me something alive and tangible and worth more than a thousand paintings. You've given me an amazing friend. You've given me... you." He hugged Armando.

They turned and looked at the painting. "I'm so glad you like it. I was very pleased with how it turned out, too. Let me get us more coffee."

Armando chuckled as he wiped his eyes. "Coffee? I think I need a drink. Yes!"

"All right! Blood Marys it is!"

As Andrew fixed the drinks, Armando got closer to the painting, examining it closely. "It is amazing. It is like looking in a mirror. Are my eyes really that green?"

"Yes, they are. Yes. They are."

"God has been so kind to let me meet and know a man such as you. How lucky am I?" Armando spoke softly.

Andrew handed him a drink and they sat down. "I'm just so glad you like it. I think it does you justice."

Armando raised his glass. "Thank you, God, for such a wonderful friend. Thank you, Andrew. I have never known such kindness and happiness. To our friendship."

Andrew raised his glass. "Thank you, Armando, for making me happy and bringing joy and friendship to this house. To our friendship."

CHAPTER X

Andrew couldn't believe how quickly time had passed. February was coming to an end. He'd have to be returning to Atlanta and his regular life again. But he couldn't dismiss how he was feeling. Feeling about Armando. He didn't want it to end. He was beginning to be afraid. Then, he would stop himself and smile. He realized what they shared would never be lost just because of distance. This house here just up the coast from Zihuatanejo would always be theirs and a refuge from the rest of the world.

They'd finished dinner and were sitting out on the terrace, watching the ocean. Andrew turned to Armando. "Okay. I know you have your life and I have mine and we both are going to have to go back to them. I have an idea. Every February we will meet here. If we can do it more often, great. But every February, we can come here and be together for one month out of the year until we get old and grey and can retire here for the rest of our lives. How does that sound?"

Armando looked directly at Andrew. "Andrew. I have something to tell you."

"Okay. We can pick another month."

"No. It has nothing to do with the month. February is just fine with me but there is something else. But I do not know how to explain it. It is the issue I have brought up several times before and has been nagging at me ever since I got here. I still have not solved the puzzle and it is driving me crazy."

"Well, out with it. Maybe I can help."

"I do not know how to explain it without it sounding ridiculous and absurd. I know it must have happened after falling off the ship and reaching the shore here. But that has not made sense to me, either, since I have gone out sailing several times and nothing changed. I know it is out there somewhere."

This was unbelievably confusing to Andrew, making no sense at all and he wasn't quite sure what to say. "Would it help if you contacted your brother in San Francisco? Maybe somewhere in your head, you're concerned about him thinking you are dead."

"No. That is not it. It is just so weird that the Fates should have it happen. Something tells me it was for a very good reason. Yes. Being here with you has absolutely changed my life for the better. But what if I get pulled back? Will I be able to get back here again?"

"Armando. This place will always be a place of refuge for you and me. Remember that. Even if I am not here, should you want to come here, do it. If you feel comfortable here, come whenever you like."

Armando just shook his head. "Yes, I know. But it just does not make sense. There has to be some key that will open the door to solve it. It is making me crazy thinking about it. I will just have to work on it and try to figure it out." He shook his head again and then smiled, looking at Andrew. "Okay. We will meet here every February. That sounds good to me. Let us go take a walk on the beach before we go to bed."

"Sounds like a winner to me. Let's go."

It was mid-morning when Armando came in to see Andrew who was working on another painting. A sunset. "I thought I would take the boat out. It looks like a great day for sailing. Maybe being out on the ocean will help me contemplate my issue and give me some insight. Since it happened out there, maybe that is where I will find the answer."

Andrew looked up from the canvas. "Okay. Have a good time and be careful. I'll see you later on this afternoon. Put on some sunscreen, so you don't burn."

"I will put it on my face. As you can see, I am wearing the jeans and a long sleeve shirt to keep my legs and arms from burning, too. See you later." Armando headed out.

Andrew called out. "Wait!" He ran up to Armando and gave him a big hug. "Thank you so much. I can't tell you how much I have so enjoyed our time together. I know it's getting closer to the time we will have to go our separate ways, so I want to take every advantage to give you a hug before that happens. Please be careful out there."

Armando smiled. "You have given me more than I could have ever imagined. To me, it is a miracle. Thank you." He hugged him, smiled as he looked at Andrew and winked his right eye. "I will be careful. Now. See you later on this afternoon." He turned and headed to the beach.

"Go out there and have some fun! I'll fix something good for dinner!" Andrew yelled out.

Andrew continued painting. He hadn't been keeping track of the time when he heard the breeze outside pick up. He looked up and out the window. He got up, went out onto the terrace then started down to the beach. He turned around and saw a big storm, coming in from over the mountains. He immediately looked out to sea, searching for Armando and the boat. He realized he must have taken it far out since it was such a beautiful day. He shook his head in questioning. "Storms are not supposed to happen this time of the year." It was very strange. "I hope he's careful out there."

Soon, the wind came down like a hurricane. Andrew ran back to the house and shut the windows in case it came a downpour then it was back out to the beach. The wind was ferocious. It headed out to sea, causing the waves to become huge mountains, crashing and pounding. Lightning flashed through the darkening sky, causing loud cracks and the booming sounds of thunder. Andrew could hear the bass kettle drums and crashing cymbals at the end of *O Fortuna* from *Carmina Burana* by Carl Orff in his mind. The storm was terrifying.

He scoured the raging sea for Armando and the boat. Nothing. He ran up and down the beach, looking out toward the horizon. Suddenly, he saw the sail. The boat was far out but it looked like Armando was trying to get it back to shore. Andrew stood there waving his arms in the air and screaming out. "ARMANDO! ARMANDO!"

The wind was relentless, blowing out to sea. Andrew could do nothing but watch. The boat was going farther and farther out, taken by the winds and waves.

Suddenly, there came a sinking feeling in his body. Immediately, he became alarmed. Would Armando be able to bring that small boat through such a storm? His heart pounded with distress. Then, came the rain. It poured down in sheets. Andrew couldn't see even beyond the close rock formations just offshore. A sense of dread made him shiver. There was nothing he could do. Armando was on his own. Andrew whispered a prayer as he stood there helpless. "Please, God, watch over him. Keep him safe." He leaned against the rock where he and Armando used to stop, during their walks on the beach. He stayed to wait out the storm.

The storm lasted about two hours then blew far out to sea. Andrew searched the horizon for the boat. He looked for hours, walking up and down the beach but there was nothing. He felt sick and returned to the terrace, sitting down, yet kept staring out to sea. Night finally fell and there was still nothing. Armando hadn't come home. Andrew sat there all night long in his wet clothes and into the early morning light, sobbing and crying.

As the day became lighter, he ran back to the beach. There was still no sign of Armando or the boat. "Maybe he pulled to shore down the beach or maybe up the beach. I have to go see."

Within minutes, he was in the Jeep and heading south. He took the turnoff toward Troncones. Reaching the beach highway there, he stopped at several places, asking if they'd seen a boat come in after the storm the day before. There was nothing positive but they would contact him if Armando turned up. Buena Vista was next. He knew it was doubtful he'd have sailed that far south but he wanted to make sure. He even went as far down as Ixtapa, asking the same. No one had seen anything.

Heading home, he was exhausted. Pulling into the garage, he got out quickly and ran down to the beach. Still, there was no sign of Armando. He had to eat something and rest. He called the airline and canceled his flight to Atlanta then called his business to tell them he wouldn't be home until he resolved a personal issue here. A shower and bed were next. It would be up the coast toward Lázaro Cárdenas in the morning.

For more than a week after the storm, Andrew constantly searched up and down the beaches. He continued to inquire miles north and south, asking if anyone had seen him, realizing he could never have sailed that far. The answer was always one he didn't want to hear. "No. Sorry. Haven't seen anyone like that on the beach. And no boat, either."

CHAPTER XI

It was now the end of the second week in March and sunset. Andrew had been out, searching all day long. Virtually two weeks of searching and there was nothing. He was getting so despondent. His whole body ached with the pain of loss.

He stood there on the sand, looking out at the sun, sinking into the horizon. He thought about the last few weeks. They'd been so incredible. Who'd have ever guessed? He'd found someone who had touched his very soul and now, he was gone. "Where can he be?" He whispered. His mind began to wonder if he could go on after what he had experienced since he first found him right here on the beach.

"Maybe he wasn't real. Maybe he didn't actually exist. Maybe he was just a figment of my imagination. They say if you're alone long enough, you start to conjure up imaginary friends." Is that what he had done? Andrew's mind kept turning it all over, again and again.

The one thing he just didn't want to face was the acceptance that Armando was dead. It seemed obvious but he just couldn't go there in his mind. He realized the sailboat in a storm like that was no match against the treacherous water and waves. There's no way the craft could have survived. It began to sink in. The sea had given Armando to him and now, it had taken him away. Tears ran down his cheeks. His heart was like a crystal goblet dropped onto a concrete pavement broken into pieces. 'All the king's horses and all the king's men couldn't put it back together again.'

He tilted his head back and let out a loud long scream of anguish then fell to his knees, sobbing and screaming out in his pain. "ARMANDO! I DIDN'T GET TO TELL YOU! I DIDN'T GET TO TELL YOU... I LOVE YOU! ARMANDO, I LOVE YOU! I LOVE YOU!" He yelled and screamed into the air then bent over pounding the wet sand with his fist. "Why? Why couldn't I have been with you? I could have died with you. It's not fair. It's not fair! First Jacob and now, you! No! No! Please, God! Don't let him be gone! Armando, I love you!"

Suddenly, there was a voice to the right of Andrew. "Andrew. Is that you?"

The voice totally startled Andrew. It sounded like Armando's. He turned quickly to his right. There, standing about eight feet away was a tall man. The golden light of the sunset made his face seem to glow and accented his black wavy hair, beard and mustache.

Andrew yelled out. "Armando! It's you! It's you!" He struggled to get up. "Oh, God! Where have you been? I've been so worried, searching for you." He tried to smile through his tears.

The man quickly approached Andrew, grabbed his arm and helped him to his feet. Andrew hugged him tightly. "Armando! I love you! I love you!"

"Andrew. No. I am not Armando." The man responded with a soft but firm voice.

Andrew slowly let go and backed away. He looked up into the man's face. "But. I don't understand. You ARE Armando. You look and sound like him. How can it not be you?" He looked hard at the man. "Oh, my God! I'm seeing ghosts! I've gone crazy! I'M SEEING GHOSTS!" He screamed out.

"No. I am not a ghost. Come. Let us go to the house and we will talk. There is much to explain." The man grabbed Andrew's shoulders. "My name is Francisco. It will be a lot clearer when we talk."

Finally, inside the house, Andrew looked with his red, teary eyes at Francisco. "Please, sit down. Can I get you some tea or coffee?"

Francisco just shook his head and smiled. "I could have expected it. From what I know of you already, you are thinking of me first, even in your adversity. What can I say? Yes. If it is not too much trouble, I would love some hot tea." He sat at the dining table. "From the writings, his description was right on the mark."

"Give me a few minutes to get the water heated up." Andrew went to the kitchen and placed the teapot on the stove. He returned to the dining room and sat down. He looked right at Francisco. "You look and sound like him. I don't understand." Tears began to roll down his cheeks. "I'm sorry. It's just that…" He bent his head down. "I hurt so bad. I miss him. And I didn't get to tell him." He put his head on the table wrapped in his arms and began to cry. "No one will understand."

"But you see. I do. I do understand. Believe it or not, I know most of everything. And many things you do not." Francisco spoke softly.

Andrew raised his head and looked across the table. "How could you? You don't know me. You don't know what I had. What I have lost. Even if it was for a short time. I know he is dead and I want to die. If you only knew the pain inside me. It was bad enough losing Jacob. Now, I lose Armando. And I didn't get to tell him… I loved him." He put his head down and sobbed. "I didn't get to tell him. I didn't get to tell him."

"He knew. Trust me. He knew." Francisco reached across the table and grabbed Andrew's arm. "Andrew. He knew you loved him."

Andrew raised his head and looked at Francisco with a questioning expression. "I don't understand. I'm really confused. If you could be in my head right now, you would think I'm going insane. Here I sit, talking to a specter, a ghost. What's funny is the ghost is talking back." He looked up to the ceiling and started to laugh through his tears. He looked right at Francisco. "Do you know how much I want to come around there, grab and hold you? But I know you will just disappear in my arms."

"Andrew. I am real but I am not Armando. I am Francisco. Did not I take your arm to help you back here to the house? I grabbed your arm just now. That should prove you can touch me. I am flesh and blood, not some specter. There is a good reason why I look like Armando and I will explain. First, you need to calm down and clear your head, so you will fully understand. I will tell you everything. It is amazing. Incredible. Unbelievable. Impossible. But it is true. It even astounds me. What I am about to tell you is going to sound virtually insane. If I were not wrapped up in it, I would think it a fantastic story of someone's imagination. Now. Let us have a cup of tea."

"Oh. Francisco. I'm so sorry. Let me fix some for you. Do you want sugar and lemon?"

"Yes. Just like Armando did." He smiled at Andrew. "This may sound weird but I am very much like him in many ways. Many ways. I did not realize it until I started researching this whole thing. To put it bluntly, the only difference between him and me is our names. We are exactly the same. Exactly." He nodded his head.

Andrew got up and fixed the tea, bringing it all to the table. He poured the cups and sat down.

Francisco looked up and twisted his mouth. "Now. Where do I begin?" He strummed his fingers on the tabletop. "Do you remember when you came down to Zihuatanejo in two thousand and four, looking to get a lot? Well. We knew you were coming. We just had to wait for it to unfold. I say 'we' but mostly me and the Vargas Law Firm as I am the one who opened the box and shook up the contents."

"What!? How did you know I came down in two thousand and four? And how could you possibly know I was coming to get property?"

"Patience. Patience. When you arrived at Manuel's office, all was in preparation. The call from Consuelo started the ball rolling. Oh, she was not involved but we knew you would go to the government land offices in Zihuatanejo first to inquire about the property. Her

E. THORNTON GOODE, JR.

call to Manuel opened the door and set all the wheels in motion. Everything was ready for you to walk into his office. It had been ready for a very long time. A very, very long time." He paused briefly before continuing. "The timeline had begun. You see. The large parcel of land was purchased some time ago in anticipation of your coming."

Andrew looked very confused. "That doesn't make sense. It sounds ridiculous. I was told by the lady at the land office the main parcel had been in the same family for over a hundred years."

Francisco shook his head. "Let me continue. Why do you think no one was able to buy a lot on the parcel? Why do you think all the land around here is still in its pristine state? Why do you think there is not another house within a mile of here?" He looked intensely at Andrew then took a sip of his tea. "Because it had to be just as it is right now. Exactly as it is right now. You and only you were to get a lot. No one else. Why do you think you got it at the price you did? Tell me you were not shocked when you were told its cost. You were supposed to have this lot. No one else. YOU."

"This is crazy." Andrew shook his head. "This sounds like..."

"Like some fantastic story from someone's imagination. Yes. I told you it would." Francisco smiled. "I knew this was not going to be easy. It took me years to put the puzzle together and understand it and here I am trying to explain it all… right now. I mean, there STILL are a few pieces missing."

"Years? You have been working on this for years? I really don't understand." A shocked and questioning expression filled Andrew's face.

"Patience. Patience." Francisco raised up his hand. "Let me continue. After my research, I knew this house and everything in it. I even know about the portraits of Jacob and Armando, hanging together there in the living room." He pointed into the darkness of the living room. "As well as the pictures of you and Armando taken on the beach, up here on the terrace and out there near the house. And the ones in on the dresser in the bedroom."

88

"How can you know? How can you know that? I have said nothing about the pictures or the paintings." Andrew put his head on the table. "It has happened. I have lost my marbles. I have gone insane. I'm ready for the booby hatch." He picked his head back up.

"No. You are not crazy. It will all make sense. Well. To you and me, it will make sense. Others may differ." He rolled his eyes. "I have to admit, I almost messed up the timeline. Here it is, the end of the second week in March. I should have been here much, much sooner. Right after Armando went sailing and the storm caused him to vanish but I was in Europe at a very important last-minute meeting and could not get here any quicker. I hope you will forgive me. Maybe if I had been here when I was supposed to be, you would not be so distraught and in such pain. Or at least, I could have been here for you to help comfort you. Andrew. I am sorry. I truly am sorry. Please, forgive me." He paused for a moment.

"Before I left Europe, I called your workplace in Atlanta to see if you had returned home. They told me you were trying to resolve some personal issue here and would not return until it was completed. That is how I knew you were still here in Mexico. Here at this house. I then contacted Manuel Vargas. He was very concerned as he knew information had to be given to you and it was way past due for delivery. I told him I was coming immediately and would pick up everything before heading out to see you. He told me he did not care when or what time but he would be there to give me everything the moment I arrived in Zihuatanejo. He wanted to make sure he fulfilled his obligation, regardless of what it took."

"Francisco. I'm so confused. You're not Armando but you look like him. You sound like him. Obviously, if you're not Armando, I don't know you. Yet you know all this and about Manuel Vargas. I have questions but I don't know what to ask much less where to begin."

"Andrew. If you knew Armando, you know me. Not my experiences but the man. I am amazed as I said. The only difference between us is our names. But let me continue."

"When I arrived in Zihuatanejo, I immediately rented a car. Manuel was waiting at his office for me to pick up the things I have here for you. Then, when I got here earlier this evening, I first came up here to the house. It was dark but your Jeep was parked in the garage, so I knew you were here. I knew you and Armando liked to walk on the beach, so that is where you had to be. That is where I found you. I came to give you something. Something very important. Something that will help you understand more of what I have told you so far. Let me go to the car and I will be right back."

Within a few minutes, Francisco returned with two large manila envelopes and placed them on the table. He first opened the one marked with a big number one and turned it up on the table. Out fell an envelope, yellow with age. A wax seal was on the closing flap. Francisco reached down and turned the envelope over.

Andrew looked down at it. On the front of the envelope was a handwritten message in black ink. 'To My Wonderful Andrew.' "What is this?" He looked at Francisco.

"It is a letter. To you."

"To me? But it looks ancient. To me? Are you sure?"

"Very sure. The personal journals explain it. This letter was updated every year, every February. And the older one thrown away. Actually, burned. No one was to ever know its contents. This was made very, very clear. The wax seal was to show that no one had tampered with it. It has been in a vault, waiting for this moment to come. This letter was to be given to you now, to explain and help you understand. Even I have no idea what is in the letter. I know everything else but not the contents of this letter."

"Seriously. It looks very old." Andrew kept staring at the letter.

"Almost a hundred years old." Francisco spoke softly. "I brought it for you to read. It is time. I will go outside if you like."

"Oh. No. Don't be ridiculous. I may have questions and you might be able to give me answers."

"Honestly. I had hoped you would let me stay. I have wanted to know what is in that letter for many years." Francisco smiled.

"But who would have written to me? Years ago?"

"That will be evident when you read it."

Andrew picked up the envelope. "Geez. I don't want to tear it open. I'll get a knife and do it carefully. This looks like something that needs to be saved for the ages." He picked up a knife from the kitchen. "I'll be very careful as I know this is very fragile." He stuck the pointed end of the knife in the corner of the sealed edge of the envelope and slowly cut the top edge, preventing the knife from going deep. He didn't want to cut or damage the letter within. That done, he slowly and carefully removed the letter. He could see there were several pages and the quality of the paper was extremely good. He unfolded it and started reading out loud, so Francisco could hear it.

"'My dearest Andrew. As you see, I do write letters. I even had special paper made to write this one and its predecessors. I told the maker the paper had to last a very long time. It is the same with the ink. I cannot tell you how many times I have written this letter to you. Every time there is just a little more to add to it. When you read further, you will see why I did not have an email address. Although, I had instructions to have an internet tower built. You will understand later. There were instructions for someone to come to you and give this letter to you the last weekend in February of two thousand and six. It would help you understand why I am not there right now with you.'"

"'I am in Zihuatanejo right now. I come here every February just like we planned. And every February, I write you another letter. Obviously, since you are reading this one, it is my last one. Every time I start one of these, tears come to my eyes. Oh, Andrew. How I miss you and I have for so many years.'"

Andrew looked up at Francisco, who only nodded and gestured to continue.

"'There is much I want to tell you, so you will understand. So, I hope you are sitting down. This could take some time. First, I must tell you that knowing you made a huge difference in my life. Our constant conversations helped me come to understand and know who I am. Knowing you made me understand how caring and considerate a person could be. I know we knew each other for only a few weeks but in those wonderful days, I learned so much about true friendship and so much more. I sometimes close my eyes and reminisce those days with you and I smile, even though tears stream down my face as they do now as I write.'"

"'I can only hope this letter will help you move on with your life. I remember our talks about your Jacob and how much you loved him. Understanding this, I came to realize I was not just a friend to you. I so hoped you knew you were not just a friend to me. I was so proud when you did my portrait and hung it next to Jacob's. My heart pounded with love and thanks. I could never have hoped for such a thing. Then, for you to tell me I was a truly handsome man and put the pictures you took of us with your camera around the house next to the ones of you and Jacob. How kind and loving of you.'"

"'I must tell you. That day. The day of the storm. I was so far out when I saw it coming in off the mountains. I turned the boat and veered toward the shore. Andrew, I saw you. You were there on the shore, waving your arms in the air. Oh, how I wanted to return to you. I tried so hard to get the boat back but the wind was too strong. It was so powerful. It pushed me farther out to sea. Soon, it was so dark and the waves so violent, I was losing the boat. I could not see the land. Suddenly, I saw a ship and it was coming my way. By the grace of God, they had seen the boat and me and came to my rescue. When I got on board, I knew instantly, I was a very long way from you.'"

"'You know that problem that was nagging at me? I finally figured it out and realized how I got to you. Somehow, it was out in the sea and connected to the storms. It could only happen during those storms. That was the key.'"

"'What you did not know has to do with the day you found me on the beach. Even I did not realize it until I saw the painting of Jacob and the date on it, the year you finished it. I was truly confused. But full realization did not hit until I saw the calendar in your kitchen. It was February, two thousand and six, not eighteen eighty.'"

Andrew looked at Francisco. "Eighteen eighty? Eighteen eighty? He is telling me he was from eighteen eighty? Oh, my God. It's beginning to make sense." He went back to the letter.

"'I had no idea how to tell you because I knew if I tried, you would think me insane and probably have fear of me. But for me, things were new and unbelievable. Yes. It all began when I awoke in your bedroom and looked around. The color pictures on your dresser. The ones of you and Jacob. Then, finally, when the electricity came back on, this was magic to me. I knew something incredible had happened. All the things I saw and found out from you in just our regular conversations. Listening to your CD player, playing music and watching old movies on your TV, using your DVD player. Your computer and telephone. If you only knew how amazing this was to me. I chuckle right now, thinking about the first time I saw your Jeep and how we went for the rides into Zihuatanejo. I can now tell you. I was terrified of it and how fast we went. But I trusted you and knew if you felt safe, it must be all right.'"

"'Zihuatanejo. Yes. The airplane at the airport. What can I say? You know, I went to Kitty Hawk in December of nineteen and three and hid behind a sand dune. I saw it happen. But I knew it would, after researching it on your computer. And the stores we went to and bought food and my new clothes. I still have the sneakers, jeans and shirt I was wearing the day I left.'"

"'I was trespassing on your time but what a time it was. What else you do not know is the ship that picked me up from the boat that stormy day, strangely was in eighteen eighty and heading to San Francisco. I had a sense because the ship was not like the cruise ship we saw, sitting in the bay that day we went to Zihuatanejo. From the masts and rigging on this ship, along with the smokestack, it was immediately obvious, I was not in two thousand and six anymore. I was back where I belonged.'"

"'I must tell you. I am sitting here laughing. You should have seen the look on my brother's face when I got off the ship and walked into his house in San Francisco. It was a very interesting reunion. Yes. It would have made you laugh, too, had you seen it.'"

"'All the things I saw. The things we talked about. The things I found out, looking through your shelf of books and on your computer, I remembered it all. That information came in very handy over the years for investments and knowing of important historical events to come. I wrote it all down in business journals, so those close to me could use the information effectively as time progressed. These were given to the family. My brothers were so amazed when I told them. At first, they were so skeptical but when they saw things come to be, things I had talked about, they understood it was not some fairytale. It made us a very wealthy family, on top of our existing wealth.'"

"'I saved my youngest brother, knowing about another event in history due to the first time you showed me how to find something by typing in the search block on your computer. He was preparing to come to the United States from Spain and had wired me by telegraph. It was early March of nineteen twelve. He had booked passage on the great new ship, coming from England. He said everyone who was anyone was going to be on board. He was going to take the train up to Cherbourg and board there.'"

"'I sent a telegram back, telling him to stay put and not get on the ship and why. Knowing my knowledge of things to come, he took my advice and came later on another ship. So, my wonderful Andrew, you not only saved my life but you saved my youngest brother's, too, from dying on the Titanic.'"

"'I must tell you. Several times, over the years, I have returned to the place where you are now. I even got a small sailboat and kept it anchored in the little cove for many years. Sometimes I would take it out and see if there was some way to return to you when I came back to shore but it was no use. Eventually, I realized it was not meant to be. The Fates meant for me to remain here in my own time. I knew this time period and how to live in it. Staying there with you in your time, I would have been a fish out of water always floundering around not understanding everything. And just as I did while I was with you, I would have constantly wondered if and when I might get pulled back to my own time and it would have weighed heavily on my mind. But I was so lucky to have had the experience with you.'"

"'In June of eighteen eighty, I came back to Zihuatanejo and bought this parcel of land north up the coast of Ixtapa. I had remembered your story. It began to make sense to me. The reason it was bought and never developed. The reason you were the only one who was able to buy a lot on it. It was because someone knew you were coming to buy and build. That person was me. All my questions were answered. I had to be the one to lay out the path for you to come to where you are. I thought a good way to do it and keep it legal and confidential would be to use a reputable law firm.'"

"'Searching, I was hearing about one that was incredible. They were noted for their fairness and honesty. They had a policy of not representing someone unless they were truly innocent. There were exceptions, cases where the action was justified or had extenuating circumstances. In those situations, they would seek a justifiable but lenient punishment. And if they represented you and found out you had lied and were guilty, they would drop you like a ship's anchor. This was definitely the type of firm I wanted. It is a wonderful law firm, run by the Vargas family, located near the bay in Zihuatanejo. But then, I remembered our conversations and realized you had used the Vargas Law Firm. I remembered you pointing in their direction when we were near the bay there. It made me smile, knowing I had chosen the correct one.'"

"'I got to talk with the head of the firm and discovered they had no problems putting up with my idiosyncrasies and wishes, especially when he found I was going to pay them well for their efforts. It was stipulated the land was to never leave the family and no one could ever buy any part of it. Only one sale would be allowed and that would take place in February of two thousand and four. I wish you could have seen the faces of those documenting the purchase, knowing it was over a hundred years in the future. It was even funnier when I told them the sale of a lot would go to only one person. A Señor Andrew Stevenson from Atlanta, Georgia in the United States. And an internet tower was to be built in two thousand and three. I am sure they thought I was crazy and had no idea what an internet tower was but no one said anything. They told me they would do everything possible to adhere to my wishes. I knew it would hold because I was there with you in two thousand and six and there were no other dwellings or structures in the area. I knew they had lived up to their promise and carried out everything perfectly. You know, the other restrictions, regarding your lot as told to you by Manuel Vargas. If you only knew how many times I have visited the spot where your house sits, closed my eyes and remembered the times there with you.'"

"'There is one other thing I would like done. I would like a small chapel built up on the bluff behind your house to hold my remains. This will be at no cost to you. I am putting monies aside for this. The reason I want this is so I can be close to you. I even insisted on being cremated and put in an urn just like the one you have with Jacob's ashes. And maybe when you join us in death, you will want to place some of your ashes in my urn just as you are going to have done with some of your ashes going into Jacob's. I would like that. Maybe you will put all our ashes together in one big urn. I am laughing right now, thinking about it happening. Then, we will all be together in the chapel. Should you meet someone special after me, you might want him to join us when he leaves this life. As you used to say, 'the more the merrier'.'"

"'It is nineteen twenty and I sit here at eighty-one years old. I will be eighty-two later on this year. Something just crossed my mind and I am snickering, thinking about how really funny it is. The portrait you did of me. It is an oil painting. The paint is still not dry as you sit reading this letter. And yet, I will have been dead for almost a hundred years. Seriously. You have to admit. That is funny.'"

Andrew looked up from reading and giggled. "You do have to admit. That is funny." He smiled and continued.

"'I hope whoever has given you this letter is sitting with you to help you understand all this. I know there is because I have a feeling you wanted him there. I hope he has some sense of humor and is not some old grouch. I hope he has some sensitivity to this whole thing. I can only hope.'"

"'The belt, cufflinks and the rings in the drawer, they are yours.'"

Andrew stopped reading and looked at Francisco. "Oh, my God. I completely forgot about Armando's belt and all in the drawer." He paused then started reading again.

"'And if you go out to that big rock just south of your terrace, there is something there for you, too. Every year I would visit here, I would leave a little something for you. I have drawn a little map for you on the last page. I know the rock is there because I saw it when I was there with you just the other day... eighty-six years from now for me. It is only a small way to thank you for everything. Thank you for showing me a great time. Thank you for being a great friend. Thank you for being so much more than a friend. Use what I have left there for you wisely. I know you will. You are so frugal.'"

"'I must be honest with you. I have met several since you. A few I had some very discreet fun with but none lasted. I was always looking for another you but no one is like you. Not in this time, anyway, with the societal mores and thinking of this time. None of them could have given me what you did. No one here could ever be as free as we were. Know I have been happy and had a wonderful life. Believe it or not, you gave me enough love and memories in those few weeks to last me the rest of my life. Thank you for that. Yes. God was kind to me and I thank Him every day for letting our lives cross. My only regret is I never told you. Andrew, my wonderful Andrew. I never told you. I never told you, I loved you. I have a feeling you knew but I so wanted to tell you. I wanted to say the words to you. But I was a little afraid. I just thought you might think it too soon, having known you for such a short time.'"

"'The way you treated me. The way you went out of your way for me. The way you cared for me. I knew you loved me. No one does things like that for just anyone. I believe you never said anything for exactly the same reason. Andrew. I say it now, here on paper. I love you. I will love you forever. Beyond death. Even now, almost a hundred years later as you read this letter, I still love you. I love you probably more than I did at forty-one when I was with you there. Andrew. I am smiling as I know you love me, too. I am telling you to do something just as Jacob told you. Find someone to love you. You deserve it. You have so much love to give. Find that someone and love him. Tell him about Jacob. Tell him about me. If he is the man I think he will be, he will be glad to know about us and understand the love you had and still have for us. He will realize and understand it does not and will not diminish the love you have for him. It is like you used to tell me. The cup of love is always full. There is enough for everyone.'"

"'By the way, do you remember the cross around my neck? Tell the person there with you, I want you to have it. He knows what I am talking about.'"

At that, Francisco opened the second envelope marked with a big number two and turned it up on the table. Out slid the gold cross and chain that had hung around Armando's neck.

Andrew continued to read. "'Well. I guess I have explained everything. Oh. Not everything. Promise me. When you play that Rosemary Clooney song, *Green Eyes*, and especially *I'll Be Seeing You*, you will think of me and remember me along with all those others you loved and cared for who are now gone from you. I can hear that song so clearly in my head as I think of you. It allows me to smile through my tears. 'I'll be looking at the moon but I'll be seeing you.'"

"'Just so you know. The pictures you gave me that I had in my wallet, they are now in frames and in my bedroom. Every time I look at them, my heart is warm and I smile. Especially, the one Hector did for me, showing the cut on my head. I look at that picture and I am there with you, taking care of me. As I told you. I have you with me, always. The ones Hector made for me I had folded. They have a few creases but they are such nice pictures. Well, I put them in a book to keep them flat. One of my journal books. It is the one with no writing in it. All these are at the Vargas Law Firm. And when I am gone, all the other pictures will be there as well.'"

"'I guess the rest can be explained by the someone there with you. Maybe you will put this letter with the portrait you did of me. It will help those in the future to maybe understand. So, I say goodbye to you. But it really is not goodbye. We will see one another again. I will always be with you and will always love you. Jacob and I are waiting for you. Take your time. There is no rush. Have a long and good life. And when it is your time, we will come for you, just like in the movie we watched. 'The Ghost and Mrs. Muir' with Gene Tierney and Rex Harrison. Andrew. I love you so much. Goodbye, my love. Adiós. Hasta luego, mi amigo. Mi amor. Armando.'"

Andrew slowly placed the letter on the table. There was silence for what seemed an eternity. Andrew's eyes filled with tears and he began to weep profusely. He'd been totally overwhelmed. Finally, after some time, he composed himself and wiped the tears away and looked across at Francisco, whose face was wet with tears and was sobbing as he stared at the letter.

Francisco looked at Andrew and his lips quivered with emotion and huge tears rolled down his cheeks. He spoke softly. "I had a feeling. But I could not imagine what Armando's letter would do to me. I now see the unbelievable and powerful love you both shared even though it was never spoken. It just reinforces all what I already know. Oh. My. God. I hurt for you both. My heart is screaming and cries out. My heart is breaking for you both."

Andrew smiled through his tears. "Francisco, no. Be happy we had what we did. Even if it was for only a few weeks. Come here."

Both men slowly stood and walked around the table toward one another, hugging each other tightly as they sobbed together, slowly swaying back and forth.

Andrew felt a strange warmth. The hug was so familiar, yet new. For some reason, he felt a kinship, an incredible connection to Francisco. He could not explain it. Finally, both men collected themselves and returned to their respective seats.

Francisco spoke softly. "That was beautiful. What a wonderful and amazing letter. I had a sense but as I said, I already had an idea he loved you with such intensity. I am astounded. Thank you for letting me hear it. It also meant so much more to hear you reading it. I now have an even greater understanding of Armando. Everyone wondered why he was a man ahead of his time. Now, I see why. Everything makes sense."

Andrew looked at Francisco. "But what is your part in this and how did you get involved?"

"Armando spoke of his two brothers. I am related to Miguel, his middle brother. I am his great, great-grandson. I think that is correct. Probably why I look so much like Armando. Relatives who knew of him and saw pictures of him have told me I am his spitting image."

"That's an understatement. Come. Let me show you." He led Francisco into the living room and turned on the lights. "See?" He pointed at the portrait.

"Amazing!" Francisco shook his head. "That is incredible." He started to chuckle. "Uncle Armando has been dead nearly a hundred years and like he said in his letter, here is his portrait, not even dry yet. Unbelievable!" He turned to Andrew. "You do realize how weird this is?" His face was filled with surprise. "I really DO look like him. What else is interesting is, I am the same age he was when he was here. I am forty-one. I will be forty-two in August."

Andrew immediately saw the humor. "I can't help it. Yes. It's so uncanny how much you look like him. Right down to his green eyes. Geez. It is weird. And the same age. Now THAT is really something." He looked at the painting then back at Francisco. "Well, I'll not see you going out into the night since it's getting rather late. You can spend the night if you like. And I'm sure you are starving if you have not had anything to eat since you left Europe."

"That would be great. It is a drive back to Zihuatanejo, especially in the dark. I do appreciate it. Please, something simple to eat. Do not go out of your way to fix something."

After a quick sandwich and some tea, it was getting time to head to bed.

"Let me go turn back the sheets in our… the bedroom. I can sleep in another bedroom."

"Andrew. Please, do not go out of your way. Please. And I do not want to put you out of your own room."

"Really. It's no trouble. I have it made up already. I have an extra toothbrush in the bathroom. Towels are in the closet there, too. Would you like another cup of tea before we turn in?"

"That would be wonderful. And if you do not mind, could you get the rings and belt Armando mentioned in his letter? I have a feeling I know what is in the belt. Unless you would rather wait until tomorrow."

"Not a problem. Let me get the kettle on the stove then I'll go get Armando's things out of our… my room."

Francisco went to the dining room and sat down while Andrew got the water started. "I'll be right back." He headed to the master bedroom and returned shortly, holding Armando's rings and cufflinks in his right hand and the thick belt in the left. He placed them on the table. "I have no idea what could be in the belt but it looks like a type of money belt to keep valuables. It's been in the drawer since Armando put it there weeks ago. Let me go get the tea poured."

Francisco put sugar and lemon in his tea and stirred it. He took a sip. "I must tell you. When I first heard the stories about Uncle Armando, I thought they were some outlandish hoax. It really began to nag at me. I had to find out for myself. But I will wait for tomorrow to explain all that. I just wanted to see if I am right about the contents of the belt. If I am right, I will tell you all about that, too." He looked down at the belt.

"Francisco. Since you seem to have a ton of time invested in all this, I think you should do the honors. I can't imagine what it could be."

"Well, thank you. But before I do, I will tell you this. If it is what I think it is, you will be able to do whatever you want, whenever you want for the rest of your life." He looked at Andrew and smiled.

A questioning look filled Andrew's face.

"We shall see." Francisco picked up the belt. It was some six inches wide with wrap-around flaps and leather ties. The way it was sewn there seemed to be six pockets in it. Francisco unwrapped the flaps and looked in. "Yep! I knew it! I was right!" He started to giggle in his pleasure of figuring it out in advance. He looked at Andrew and smiled. "I was right." He carefully turned the belt upside down. With some coaxing, the contents of the pockets started to emerge and roll out onto the table. There were five very large stones and a multitude of smaller ones. "Now, do you understand what I meant about being able to do what you want when you want?" He smiled.

Andrew's eyes grew wide and his mouth opened in awe. He looked at Francisco. "Oh, my God!! Are they real? You have to be kidding me. And I thought the stones in his rings and cross were something to see. Francisco. These stones must be worth a fortune."

"THAT is a definite understatement. But I will tell you more tomorrow. I am really tired. I have been traveling what seems like forever to get here. I hope you do not mind."

"I'm so sorry. Yes. You've traveled all the way from Europe and I know you're exhausted. Yes. Go to bed. We can talk tomorrow."

Francisco headed to the master bedroom. "Goodnight, Andrew."

Andrew smiled. "Goodnight, Francisco. And sleep as long as you like. I know you really are tired." He walked down the hall to the second bedroom, removed his clothes and got in bed.

Not long afterward, Francisco yelled out. "Goodnight, John Boy!"

They both roared with laughter.

"I will explain that one tomorrow, too!" Francisco yelled.

Andrew continued to giggle, peered up into the darkness, closed his eyes, smiled and spoke softly. "I love you, Armando. And thanks for sending Francisco. I know you had a hand in this. I realize you knew I would like him. He seems to be a lot like you. You're right. I do like him. I really like him. Thank you, Armando. Thank you, my love."

CHAPTER XII

Andrew had been up for over an hour, getting things ready to fix breakfast. He understood Francisco sleeping late. Many years earlier he'd traveled to Europe but the coming back was a real wipe-out. It seemed like the day would never end. He remembered being totally exhausted by the time he finally went to bed that night.

Shortly, Francisco appeared from around the corner. "I am so sorry about sleeping so long."

"Hey. I get it. Did it once years ago. I do remember. This thing about arriving at virtually the same time you took off due to the time zones and you'd been flying for over six hours. Longest day of my life. Yeah. I remember it well. And yours was worse, I'm sure. Especially, if you had to go through Mexico City. Hey! I swear. That is a workout just by itself. Okay. Breakfast! Hope you like eggs. I'm fixing an omelet for us."

"Oh. Thanks. I love a good omelet."

"Here's your coffee. I took the liberty of putting hazelnut creamer in it. Armando liked it that way."

"Hmmm. Maybe that is why I love hazelnut in my coffee." Francisco gave a 'thumbs up'.

Andrew looked at Francisco for a second and shook his head. "I swear. Hmmm."

Andrew placed the plates on the table and sat down. Just as he did, he saw Francisco bend his head, cross himself and was quiet for a moment. Then, he crossed himself again, looked up at Andrew. "I hope you do not mind. It is just I like to take a few moments to be thankful for all I have and how lucky I have been."

"I think it's wonderful. Armando said virtually the same thing. I definitely agree. We should give a few seconds of thanks for all we do have." He paused for a moment. "And have had. We should continue to do it."

After eating, Andrew poured more coffee and sat down at the table across from Francisco.

It gave Francisco his opening to start. "I know you are wondering how I already know so much. Very easy. After hearing the stories about Uncle Armando, I could not resist checking into it all. Everyone in the family had basically put it all to rest but not me. I just had to know. It reminds me of a phrase that used to be on one of those old Hollywood tell-all papers, 'The National Enquirer', you used to see in racks in grocery stores. 'Enquiring minds want to know.' Well. I had an 'Enquiring mind' and I wanted to know." He shook his head and giggled. "Actually, I think that scandal paper is still in print. Not sure as I have not looked for one in years."

"First of all, I went to the big vault located in Acapulco. It is in Armando's house there. I thought it would be as good a place as any to start my quest. The family had been using the house as a recreational place for ages. I remembered from when I was much younger, there seemed to be some possibly interesting things stored there."

"After a few days of looking, I realized, or so I thought, there really was nothing in it with regards to what I wanted to know. Just a few land maps, books following the care and maintenance of the Acapulco house and its staff as well as the houses in Madrid and San Francisco, inventory of things in the houses, family stuff and some cash. Actually, lots of cash. It was like a personal bank for when family members came to the area. Everyone would bring cash and put it there. If they did not use it all, it would build up for the future."

"But then, I came across one document that was intriguing to me. It was a document from one of the banks in Europe, regarding a very old law firm in Zihuatanejo. It made reference to the law firm and a piece of property north up the coast from Ixtapa. The letter indicated it had paid the recent annual legal fees for overseeing the maintenance, the paying of the taxes and care of the property. Looking closer, I saw there were many of these letters in a box, stuck in the back of the vault, going back for years and years. All I could figure out is one of the family members or one of the accountants must have opened them and placed them in the vault every year."

"I was sure other members were so involved with their end of the family businesses, they could not be bothered with a paltry sum being paid to some seemingly minor law firm in Mexico. But not me. I was curious. I had never heard of this law firm. Now, remember, this was some twenty years ago."

Andrew blurted out. "Twenty years ago!? You have to be kidding me! You've been involved with this for twenty years?"

Francisco grinned. "Yep. Once I started, I could not stop. Every time I was about to drop it, something kept me going forward. What can I say? And it is not like I did not have the time."

"Not to sound like some spoiled little rich kid but I had finished my education through boarding schools and higher learning in Europe and I did have time on my hands. This research would be my adventure, my quest to get to understand my long-dead Uncle Armando who I kept being told I looked so much like him. I decided to visit the law office in Zihuatanejo. It was in nineteen eighty-six when I was twenty-one."

"I drove up to the offices and walked in. They had no idea who I was. I asked to speak with the man whose name was on the door about one of their clients. I did expect the receptionist to tell me I was going to have to make an appointment but she got up and asked me to please wait. She went down a hall and was gone for several minutes."

"When she returned, there was a stocky Hispanic gentleman who looked to be in his early fifties, walking behind her. He walked up to me and smiled. I stood up and we shook hands. 'Señor, my name is Enrique Vargas. I am head of this law firm.' Suddenly, he shook his head as if trying to remove old cobwebs to remember a long-lost memory. Then, a questioning look came to his face."

"'Señor Vargas, how are you? I am Francisco de Santiago.' I smiled, trying to return pleasantries but he kept staring at me like he was seeing something he should not be seeing. Suddenly, he seemed to beam. '¡Señor de Santiago! Please, come into my office. Welcome.' I have to admit, it was like he had suddenly met some long-lost relative."

"We went into his office and sat down. I told him to please call me Francisco." Francisco looked at Andrew and shook his head. "That… is when it began."

"Enrique stood and pulled out an old book from his bookshelf. Continuing with cordial conversation about the weather and where I was staying, he kept going through that book, flipping through the pages. Finally, he stopped and looked intently at the place where he had stopped. Then, he looked at me and shock covered his face. Sitting down, he was quiet for a few moments."

"'Señor, I would like to know. Did you have a relative in your family who lived in the last century whose name was Armando?' I have to admit, I was taken aback a bit but then realized the family bank account was paying them every year for overseeing a piece of property. But for him to ask about Armando directly was a bit unsettling."

"I smiled and told him I did. He was an uncle who had died sixty-some years earlier. Enrique crossed himself then looked at me. 'Señor Francisco, now do you see why I could not believe my eyes?' He pulled two old photographs from the pages of the book he had been looking at and placed them on the desk next to one another in front of me. Yes. The man in the pictures looked like me but was older. I knew they were professional pictures of Uncle Armando but wasn't sure how or why Enrique had them. I looked closely at the pictures and could see they had once been folded. On one of them, I saw there was like some large scar on the forehead. I could not understand why a professional photographer had not removed the mar like he had on the other one."

"Seeing the pictures, I began to understand his reactions to me. Then, I explained I was there to get information about Armando, trying to find out more about who he was and what his connection was with the law firm."

"'Señor Francisco, I would like to have my son, Manuel, in on this conversation since he will be the one who will be taking this account over after me.' He left the room but was back very shortly accompanied by a young man who looked to be about thirty-two. Maybe thirty-three. After introductions, we sat down and began talking."

"'To fully understand the account, I must start at the beginning.' Enrique pointed at the old pictures of Armando. 'Señor Armando came to our office virtually a hundred years ago in eighteen eighty. He indicated he needed the services of a law firm that would do exactly what he desired and have the strictest of privacy and confidentiality. The account he wanted to establish would go way beyond his years as well as all those present at the time. After he set down stringent rules, our firm decided we would be glad to help him.'"

"'It started with the purchase of a parcel of coastal property that presently is located north of Ixtapa and Zihuatanejo. He wanted us to acquire the property for him and continue to maintain it. Whatever was necessary regarding it would take top priority. Nothing could happen to it. The firm was to submit an annual expense report to a bank in Switzerland where an account would be established for these expenses and reimbursements. Another bank would have a special account to pay them retainer fees every year. This would be done quarterly. At that, he placed ten thousand American dollars on the desk. I understand he smiled and made the comment he thought it should be enough to get things moving.'"

Francisco looked at Andrew. "You do realize ten thousand dollars in eighteen eighty was one hell of a lot of money." He flexed his eyebrows and continued.

"Enrique continued. 'What really got everyone startled were the restrictions he demanded for the property. Not one square meter of the property could ever be sold, not until the month of February in the year two thousand and four.' He looked at me with a huge grin on his face. 'You do realize that is eighteen years from now. Can you imagine what they thought about that back in June of eighteen eighty?'"

Francisco shook his head. "Of course, you can imagine my thinking as well as the expression on my face at the time. But I did not question him. I just kept listening."

"Enrique continued. 'Armando's next comment made everyone think he was crazy but it did not matter. He was our client and we said we would carry out his wishes. He indicated in that month, a man named Andrew Stevenson from Atlanta, Georgia, in the United States, would come, asking about the possible purchase of a lot. Then, and only then the lot he indicated was to be sold to him for a tenth of its value at the time. An excellent builder and architect in the area would be provided for him and his home completed in a timely fashion. All property taxes, trust fees and all the maintenance costs and other fees would be paid by the firm.'"

"Enrique then chuckled. 'One thing no one understood was when he talked about the construction of an internet tower high on the parcel in the year two thousand and three. Of course, no one knew what he was talking about but he told them to write it in the instructions for the property. It would be understood what it was at that time. The firm would be reimbursed by the Swiss account.'"

"'The firm would continue to pay these fees and continue to do so until the death of Andrew Stevenson or the death of any spouse or partner he might have at the time. At no time could the property be sold to anyone outside the family. If for some reason he needs or wants to sell the property, he would have to sell it back to the family at the fair market value of the property at that time. After the time, Andrew and his spouse or partner passed away or spouse or partner of Andrew's spouse or partner passed away, then and only then could parcels on the property be sold. They said Armando laughed, saying he already knew the property would never be sold but he was not taking any chances. Again, everyone wondered if he was some medium who could foretell and see the future but no one wanted to ask.'"

"Now, you know I was astonished at this revelation. I now understood the letters I had found in the vault in Acapulco. There was no other member of the family who had any clue, regarding all this. I had turned over a rock no one had ever seen before. But Enrique's story was just beginning. He had so much more to tell about Armando."

Francisco continued. "Enrique turned to Manuel. 'Manuel. Please go to the vault and bring the large box to me that has the name of Armando de Santiago on it.' Manuel left the room. Enrique looked at me. 'I can see this is something I am sure you never expected. We have tried very hard to keep our end of the bargain in this whole matter. We do have to stay on our toes as the bank that pays the quarterly fees, which I might add are quite substantial and very adequate and handsome, comes and does a periodic audit, totally unannounced. But we understand. From the beginning, we saw this was going to be a very good account but it was going to be an extremely unusual one.'"

"Enrique looked up in the air with a searching expression on his face. 'I think it was my great-grandfather who was head of the firm then. I was told he and Armando became very good friends as they were around the same age. It seems every time he came to Zihuatanejo, he and my great-grandfather would visit and talk. I believe that is why he entrusted us with what you are about to see. With our promise of confidentiality, we could never speak openly about this to anyone for fear we would lose the account. I must tell you. When I first saw some of the items, I was so shocked and there was no explanation for what I was seeing. I could only accept it. I believe you will understand when you see for yourself. I see you are a relative of Armando's but we cannot let any of the items I am going to show you leave the premises. Part of the agreement is that they stay in the vault at all times.'" He paused for a moment. "'Well. There are three items that are allowed to leave when the time is appropriate. But you will know this shortly.' He left the room for a short period then returned with a bronze urn. He handed me the urn."

"Needless to say, I was rather surprised as well as confused. It contained the ashes of Uncle Armando. Why would my Uncle Armando have his ashes put in an urn and placed in a vault to be kept for a hundred years? Somehow, this raised my curiosity even more and made me want to know even more about the whole thing."

"Manuel finally entered the room and placed a very large box on the desk. 'Papito. We should go to the conference room as it may be easier to examine the items?' We headed to the conference room."

"Manuel opened the box and waited. Enrique spoke. 'Señor Francisco, please.' He pointed at the box. 'The urn was one of the three items I spoke of. The other two are in the box along with an empty leather wallet and several framed pictures. Armando wanted all these as well as his personal journals placed in the vault and kept in confidence after he passed away.'" Manuel and Enrique took a seat.

"I looked in the box and saw many items. There was a smaller box labeled 'PICTURES'. I pulled this out and opened it. Inside were a number of small framed pictures. I carefully pulled out the contents as I could see they were very old and placed them on the table. They were old color photographs, faded by time. I shook my head as it did not make sense. I saw myself in the pictures. In some, there was another man. If they belonged to Uncle Armando, these were color photos before they were ever in existence."

Francisco looked at Andrew. "The other man in the pictures was... you. But of course, I did not know that at the time."

Andrew interrupted. "The pictures I took with my camera. I knew he had them. But why did he want them kept in that vault?"

"Patience. I am getting there." Francisco continued. "I looked at Enrique and Manuel with surprise all over my face. 'Now, do you see why I was so shocked?' Enrique spoke out. 'I had seen the photos when my father turned the account and this box over to me and explained the story behind it all. I am still shocked. Because I know the man in the photo is not you but is Armando. And if you look at this photo, you will see something that presently does not exist.' He pointed to a house in the background. 'I have been to that property many times and I recognize the spot. But there is no house on that spot right now. Yet, there is a photo of Armando and another man, standing on the beach in front of it. If you look at one of the other pictures you can see the house again. I know who the other man is. I know from the personal journals that are stored in the other boxes in the vault, written by Armando. It may not seem rational but that man is Andrew Stevenson and that is his house. It will be built in the year, two thousand and four.'"

"You could have knocked me over with a feather. I was speechless. I tell you now, I came out here several times just to see for myself. I recognized specific rock formations and the mountains in the background. And by God, the place where there was a house in the pictures had nothing on it except vegetation. It wasn't until eighteen years later when Manuel called me, in two thousand and four, I realized everything I had read about in the personal journals had begun here in Mexico. I believe Armando wanted the pictures kept in the vault for safekeeping and to shed light on the validity of his demands for the future."

"I reached in the big box and pulled out a large jeweled cross on a chain. I looked at Enrique who looked at the cross and responded. 'That was Armando's. He wants it to go to Andrew while the letter to him is being read by him.' I placed the cross on the table. Next, I saw an old envelope with writing on it. 'To My Wonderful Andrew.' I was so careful, removing it and putting it on the table."

"Enrique looked at the envelope. 'No one is allowed to open it. Part of his wishes. That letter is to be given to Andrew the last weekend of February in two thousand and six. It will explain everything to him. It is all in the personal journals in the other boxes. We have them in the vault. They begin in eighteen eighty and end in nineteen twenty when Armando died at the age of eighty-two. Being our client, I felt it necessary to know what we were holding and its importance, so I read all the journals. You will find them very interesting. We will keep them in the vault here but I want you to feel free to come anytime and go through all these things. I think you should read the journals. You will find them extremely fascinating.'"

"'In all these years, we have never had a member of the family ever come by, regarding Armando or his things. You are the first. I think he would not mind you knowing what we do and to read his words and see his things. I guess no one was concerned about any of it. It is rather sad because from what I know of the man, he was a fine gentleman, extremely generous and kind.' Enrique looked at me and smiled. 'I think it fitting that a man, who is a relative much less his own image, be the first to visit and ask about him. I sometimes think the Fates work in strange and mysterious ways. It was his last desire, as I have mentioned in his last will and testament, to have all the things we have here placed in our vault until the appropriate time. Maybe in twenty more years, you will be the one to deliver the letter to Andrew Stevenson.' Enrique chuckled. 'I am sure it may give him cause to pause. And with regards to his remains in the urn, again, at his request upon death, there is some statement in his will, indicating their final resting place would be realized sometime in two thousand and six. I am not exactly sure what that means but something tells me there are instructions or requests written in that letter. We will not know for another twenty years. What can I say?'"

"I had to laugh inside myself as I scratched my head. This was something totally out of an episode of *The Twilight Zone*. Too bad Rod Serling did not know about this one. He would have had a field day with it."

"Eventually, I got to read all the journals. And what a tale they told. Andrew. His personal journals were totally unvarnished. He expressed his heart and soul in them, explicitly and in detail. And you were all over them. He wrote of an amazing and unbelievable love. Through his words, I came to know you and strangely, I came to have a love for you as well. One day you will have to read them. They are the story of an incredible friendship and love over the years, through time, knowing they would never meet again, not until death. They were wrenching and heartbreaking at times. I cannot tell you how many times I had to stop reading because I was crying so profoundly. What an enormous love he had for you. I also understood why Armando had those journals and his pictures put away in the vault at the law firm. He had no desire for any of the family to know about them until it was time. Now. It was hearing his last letter to you that put the final touches to the end. That is why I could not help but get emotional when you read it. I understood. The photos Enrique pulled from that book he first opened in the office those many years before. The ones he placed on the desk in the beginning. The one without the mar on his head was the same professional one you have framed and sitting on the table in the living room. Of course, the ones in the office had aged tremendously."

Andrew sat there in total astonishment. It explained why Manuel had looked at him so strangely that first meeting in his office. The pictures in the book were the ones taken by Hector just a few weeks ago and the color photos were the duplicate ones he'd given Armando to keep. The empty wallet was the one he'd bought for Armando. Everything was coming into clear focus. What was also clear is he missed Armando that much more. "I did love him. I loved him so much. I thought I was never going to love again after Jacob but then, there was Armando. And he is gone. I feel like I could die."

Francisco responded. "You remember what he said. He told you to find someone to love you. That you deserved to be loved. He would want that and I know Jacob would as well."

"Wow. I don't know about you but I could use a Bloody Mary." Andrew shook his head and took a deep breath. "This truly is something extremely difficult to get one's head around. Damn."

"I would love one. Thanks. And, yes. You are so right there."

Andrew got up to get the drinks. "Maybe one of these days I can go see Manuel and see Armando's things. And I can read the journals. Maybe they will let me bring Armando's urn back here, so I can put it with Jacob's."

"Now, I can tell you about the jewels from the leather belt."

"I hope you don't mind but can that wait for another day. I have been totally overwhelmed right now. I need time to let all this settle if you don't mind."

"Great! Let us go walk on the beach for a while." Francisco suggested.

"Terrific. Let me pour a jug of Bloodys to take with us."

They kept going over so many of the things Francisco had talked about earlier, during their walk. Andrew just kept turning everything over in his head, again and again. What was so amazing is he was in love with a man from another century. To him, it just proved that love knows no boundaries, not even the one of time. It felt good to have Francisco there.

Andrew turned to him. "Thanks for being here. It really helps to have you here. Somehow, with you here, it's like I have an incredible connection back to him."

Francisco smiled. "I am glad to be here. I would not have had it any other way."

After several hours on the beach, they started up to the house. "Can I help you with dinner?" Francisco asked.

"Not to worry. You're my guest. Thought we could have steaks on the grill. How does that sound?"

"I love it. While you are getting things started in the kitchen, I will get the grill started."

"It's a deal. And afterward, we can watch an old movie."

"It sounds good to me." Francisco headed to the terrace to start the grill and Andrew went to the kitchen.

After a while, Andrew called out. "How did you know about the 'John Boy' thing?"

"It is all there. In the journals. Armando never understood the true humor of what it meant but when I read it, I howled out loud. I used to do the same thing when I was in college with my roommates. I used to watch reruns of old TV shows and knew what it was. I still think it is funny."

CHAPTER XIII

As Andrew left his bedroom, he saw Francisco coming from the master bedroom. He stretched his arms in the air. "Good morning!"

"And to you, too." Francisco gave a wide yawn.

"Did you sleep all right?"

"Like a rock. Thanks."

"Ready for some coffee?"

"Sounds good to me."

Francisco sat at the table. Andrew went to fix breakfast. They had been rather quiet until Andrew spoke. "I really have to call and see what's happening with the business. I was supposed to be back there like two weeks ago. But I shouldn't worry. They are very competent and know what they're doing. Guess I'm lucky to have great employees. But I guess they should know I haven't dropped dead."

Francisco snickered. "Funny. I have no idea. I kind of play at business. Not actual playing while at one of the businesses but I think the right word is 'dabble'. Yes. I 'dabble' at business. We have so many employees who do the real work and then folks to make sure THEY are doing everything right. The family is like an ornamental figurehead and getting paid quite well, I should say."

Andrew brought the eggs, bacon and toast to the table. Conversation stopped for a while until they finished eating. Andrew removed the plates and poured more coffee.

E. THORNTON GOODE, JR.

Andrew started the conversation again. "Armando said the family was in banking and jewelry. He said they had been doing it for a long time."

"If you consider doing it from the time of the Middle Ages a long time, then, yes. It truly started with the jewelry end. We would go to the places in the world where we knew precious gems were being discovered, starting small mining operations. Because of middlemen, shell companies and confidential holdings, only a handful of people truly realized we have furnished many of the major gems in the world. They are in the crowns, scepters and around the necks of many kings and queens around the world, both past and present. You know all those Fabergé Eggs and pieces of jewelry made for the Russian Czars?"

"Wow! Really? I saw the collection that's at the Virginia Museum of Fine Arts. It was donated by Lillian Pratt back in the forties. It's supposed to be the largest collection of Fabergé outside Russia. Holy Cow!"

"And speaking of gems, I need to tell you about these." He looked at the ones still lying on the table. There were three very large cut and polished gems that were obviously diamonds, one large green stone and one very large red one. There were ten other smaller ones but they were not that small in Andrew's eyes. Francisco separated the stones then began to talk about them."

"These three are diamonds." The stones glittered in the light. "This one is around one hundred and thirty-five carats. This one is one hundred. And this one is about one hundred and ten carats. The ruby here is almost two hundred. The emerald is around one hundred and twenty. Armando had them securely in the pockets. The smaller are diamonds, rubies and emeralds. Mostly diamonds as you can see. They range between ten and thirty carats each."

"No wonder Armando had them strapped to his stomach. Good place to hide them as well as keep from losing them. Hell yeah. And he wants me to have them? They have to be worth a small fortune." He looked at the collection again. "Or should I say a HUGE fortune?"

"Armando was the first son and the one to get the major inheritance, not that the other brothers were left out in the cold. Far from it. But the big family jewels always went to the first son." Francisco paused, thinking about what he had just said and started to blush, looking at Andrew. He bent his head down to hide his huge smile and started to snicker.

Andrew, hearing the comment, formed a smile that grew into a big grin and then both started laughing, louder and louder. "Family jewels! Big family jewels! He got the big family jewels!" They couldn't stop laughing. As they began to calm down, Andrew spoke slyly. "Yeah. Trust me. He had some nice 'family jewels'. Oh! Did I say that?" He looked at Francisco and they both burst into raucous laughter again. Andrew looked up in the air and put his hands together. "Forgive me, Armando. I'm sorry. But I just know you're laughing right along with us."

"Ah, hmmm. Where was I before I was so RUDELY interrupted?" Francisco chuckled and shook his head. "Glad to see you DO have a sense of humor. Makes me like you even more."

"Okay. I've got to have a glass of iced tea." Andrew got up and headed to the fridge.

"I hope you are fixing me one, too." Francisco snickered, then winked his right eye.

"Hell yeah." Andrew couldn't believe what he'd just seen. It was exactly what Armando used to do. It made him smile and feel warm inside. Francisco truly was so very much like Armando.

"These stones are worth a great deal of money. When I said you could do anything you wanted, I meant it. You do not ever have to work again. You can oversee your business like I do and travel, paint, anything you want."

"I'm sure the family must have wondered where they have been all these years. I mean, if I knew such things were part of a family heritage, I sure as hell would have liked to have had some idea as to where they were."

"Yes. No one questioned their location until after Armando died. But there was no information as to what he had done with them. Searches were made through bank vaults and other locations across the globe where he may have stashed them but to no avail. Yes. Everyone knew of their value but thought they would turn up one day. I mean, it was not like you could sell such stones and not be noticed. And there were only so many people in the world who could afford to buy such gems. If that had happened, you know there would have been a major inquiry as to how they had been obtained by the seller. The family's wealth was never tied to them, either. Their value was a drop in the bucket compared to the existing family wealth. And it had been growing greatly with what Armando had written down in business journals and given to the family to review for future investments. These business journals, unlike the ones in the Vargas offices, did not contain anything about his personal and private writings. Just business stuff."

"Well, I have to return the gems to the family. They should stay in your family, not mine. They are part of your heritage and legacy. I know Armando meant well but seriously, they should stay in the family. His cross, too."

Francisco looked hard at Andrew. "He meant every word. That is how much he loved you. They are yours."

"Okay. I have an idea. See if it's an option. How about I give the gems back to the family and if there is enough money available to cover their value, put that in a trust for me and the trust can pay me a sum maybe every quarter? That way I get the use of the value of the gems and the family would have them back again." He grinned and held his arms out like a balance, each hand, palms up in the air. He tipped back and forth.

Francisco shook his head and smiled. "Strange. I was going to suggest the same thing."

"If I could keep the cross, I would like that, so I could wear it." Andrew stopped short. He stood and picked up the cross. He smiled, holding the cross to his mouth, kissing it then speaking softly into it. "Armando. I love you so." He held it away from himself, looking hard at it. Then, he walked around the table and placed it around Francisco's neck. He looked into Francisco's face and caressed it with both hands. He quietly spoke. "No. I should not wear it. You should have it. Wear it. I believe God made you look like him for a reason. You say the cross is mine which means I can do with it as I please. And I wish you to have it and wear it. That would please me."

Francisco stood and hugged Andrew. "Armando could not have been more correct about you and how kind and thoughtful you are."

"Maybe we should check out the other thing he mentioned in his letter." Andrew picked up the letter from the table and pulled out the last page. "This is a drawing of the house here and the rock out near the terrace."

"Are you sure the rock has not been disturbed?" Francisco was unsure.

"When I first saw this property back in two thousand and four before the house was built, that rock was right where it is now. It has never been moved. I mean it's enormous and too damn heavy to move. From the drawing, there are several 'X' marks on the far side of the rock. There's also a comment about 'three feet'. I guess Armando put something there and three feet under the ground. Let's go check it out. I have a small shovel in the garage. Jacob bought it to do some landscaping. Just a second." Andrew headed out to the garage and was back shortly.

They walked out over the terrace and to the far side of the big rock there. Andrew ran back to check again the drawing in the letter still lying on the table. He returned to the rock. "Looks like this should be the spot. I think I'll dig a trench along this side just to make sure I don't miss anything." He started digging a trench about two feet wide and then down. "Damn. Three feet is not very shallow."

"I am sure he did it to make sure it would not be disturbed." Francisco replied. "Here. Let me help." He took the shovel from Andrew and started digging. He finally hit something. "There is something here. I want to be careful. It might be rather fragile after all these years."

"Let me go get a garden trowel. We can be more careful with it than the shovel."

"That is a great idea."

Soon, Andrew returned with the garden trowel and was digging around the spot where Francisco had hit something. It was soon evident. It was an old, rotten, wooden box. The minute Andrew started digging around it, it began to fall apart. Then, the contents became very clear. The sunlight glinted off them. "Gold coins. It's a bunch of gold coins." Andrew picked one up. "It's a twenty-dollar gold piece." He turned the coin in his hand. "It's dated eighteen eighty-two." He grabbed up a few more and placed them on the ground near the hole.

Francisco picked up a few. "Yes. They are all twenty-dollar gold pieces. This one is dated eighteen seventy-six and this one eighteen seventy-eight."

Andrew continued to remove the dirt carefully, so as not to cover up any of the treasure. While he dug, Francisco started removing the coins.

"Francisco, go get the little plastic bucket from the garage. We can put the coins in that for now. Take and put them on the dining table."

In about four hours, they had dug a trench almost ten feet long and three feet wide. Several old and very deteriorated wooden boxes were found. All were full of gold coins. Francisco carefully dumped several bucket loads on the table. "Andrew. Let us go organize the ones we have already. We can come back and get the rest."

"Good idea. They're not going anywhere."

Andrew got a few hand towels from the bathroom closet and they started wiping and stacking them in groups of ten. Within the hour, they had a square of ten rows by ten rows and a few more stacks. There were one thousand and thirty-seven coins. Andrew looked at Francisco. "There's over twenty thousand dollars in coins here so far."

"Actually, you have significantly more than twenty thousand." Francisco smiled.

Andrew looked strangely at Francisco.

"Do you know how much one of these coins, over a hundred years old, could possibly fetch on the coin collector's market? Not to mention the value of the gold that is in the coins."

"Oh, crap! I never thought about that."

"I will bet Armando did. Trust me. From what I know of him, he was a very shrewd and smart man. Yes. I can see he wanted to make sure you had no financial problems for the rest of your life. And we have not found all the coins yet."

Andrew clapped his hands. "This calls for a drink. How about a Whiskey Sour? I don't care if it's only two-thirty. Hey! As Alan Jackson and Jimmy Buffett would say, 'It's five o'clock somewhere'." Andrew shook his head and went to fix the cocktails.

"Sounds good to me." Francisco obliged. "Okay. Now, that you have immediately become a multimillionaire, what do you plan to do with it?"

"Damn! You're right!" He handed Francisco a glass. "I don't have to work anymore. I can travel. I can go see all those places I've wanted to see and the museums and monuments. The Gothic cathedrals, Versailles, the Hermitage, the Louvre." He looked at Francisco. "But what about my business?" He joined Francisco at the table.

Francisco smiled. "As I suggested. Let them run it. Seriously. You said they are competent. You can check up on them now and then and if you want to do some final touches on something, you can. As for traveling, you can tell me things you are interested in seeing. I have been virtually everywhere worth seeing in my life.

Maybe you will let me show it all to you." He flexed his eyebrows, grinned and winked his right eye.

"Oh, Francisco. That would be so much fun. And you would want to travel with me? Really!? I know we could have a blast. Damn. Don't anyone pinch me. I don't want to wake up." Andrew looked up into the air and closed his eyes. "Armando, thank you. Thank you so much for what you've done for me. Bless you. I hope Jacob gives you a big hug for being so kind to me." He looked over at Francisco. "What if I fill a jug and we go walk on the beach. I really need all this to sink in."

"Do you not want to see about the rest of the coins out there?" Francisco was curious.

"They'll be there later, tomorrow, whenever." Andrew gave a big grin. "And I'm not sure the table can take much more weight of all that gold." He began to chuckle.

Francisco agreed. "You are right there. I think a walk would be great."

"And when I have a few cocktails and get halfway to La La Land, we can come back and I'll fix dinner. Something easy." Andrew gave a 'thumbs-up'.

Francisco clapped his hands. "And while you fix dinner, I will clear all these coins and jewels off the table and put them away for you in one of the closets."

Andrew added. "And regarding Armando's rings. Just so you know. Those should go back to the family as well."

For about four hours, they walked on the beach, talking about the coins, jewels and how Andrew wanted to spend the rest of his life. Every time he mentioned a place he wanted to see in the world, Francisco indicated he'd been there and how much fun it would be to share it with Andrew. He also said he knew it would be interesting to see many of the places and things through new eyes. With Andrew's background in art and architecture, he most likely would be filled with additional information.

By the time they returned to the house, the jug of Whiskey Sours was empty. Grilling a steak and fixing a quick salad would be the menu for the evening. Andrew fixed another big jug of Whiskey Sours after dinner to keep in the fridge for another time. Francisco had cleared a place in the closet on the floor and put all the coins there. He put the jewels back in the leather belt and placed it and the jewelry in the nightstand next to the bed where they originally were.

After eating, they went to sit in the living room. Andrew refreshed their drinks and handed one to Francisco before sitting down.

"Armando said you have a really good collection of movies. You have no idea how much he enjoyed watching them, especially the ones that were romantic. It always made him glad they all ended with the people in love, living happily ever after."

Andrew was surprised. "Would you like to see one? Certainly, we can watch one."

"One he seemed to like a lot was called 'The Enchanted Cottage'. He wrote about it in his journals. It made him feel good that the characters had the ability to look beyond their lack of physical beauty and see the love within."

"I love that movie, too. Regardless of how many times I watch it, it still makes me cry." Andrew got up. "Let me go put it on and let's get comfortable."

As 'The End' appeared on the screen followed by the RKO Radio Pictures logo, both Andrew and Francisco had tears rolling down their faces. Francisco spoke softly. "Armando was right. It does have a powerful message. And the story told by the old lady about the secret of the cottage was amazing. What a wonderful movie. I hope we can watch more of them if they are like that one."

"Hey. You are speaking to a true romantic here. I have always believed that love will out. At least it's a nice thought." Andrew smiled. "Well, I guess it's time to hit the hay."

"I guess you are right."

"I have an idea for tomorrow. We will have to ride into Zihuatanejo."

"Sounds like a plan to me." Francisco winked his right eye.

Andrew got into bed and lay there thinking how much he was enjoying Francisco's company. He smiled. He really liked him. It was uncanny how much he was like Armando.

He was just about to fall into slumber when he heard his bedroom door open. Even in the darkness, he knew it was Francisco walking over to his bed. "Francisco, is everything all right?"

Francisco spoke softly. "I know this may seem presumptuous of me but I want to sleep with you. If I am stepping out of bounds, I understand and I am sorry. I will go back to my room."

Andrew was surprised but thought it might be nice to have Francisco there. It would be comforting. "Francisco. Come, get in bed. It would be nice to have you here."

Francisco got in and his arm went over and around Andrew pulling him close. The only sound was that of the crashing waves out on the rocks and beach. Soon, they were asleep.

CHAPTER XIV

Andrew woke up and found Francisco's arm still around him. He'd slept so well. It took him back to the times with Jacob and Armando. There was such a feeling of contentment, everything being as it should be and he liked it. He eased out of the bed.

Andrew had been fixing breakfast when Francisco came around the corner and smiled. "Good morning. I hope you slept as well as I did."

"Actually, I slept very well, thank you." Andrew placed the plates on the table and poured the coffee. "Do me a favor. When we finish eating, go pick out one of the Guayaberas in the closet and wear it today. I know you'll look great in one."

Within the hour, they were in the Jeep, heading into Zihuatanejo. Andrew hadn't told Francisco the destination. Finally, they pulled up in front of the shop owned by Hector and María. He looked over at Francisco with a big grin on his face. "We're here. Mister DeMille. It's time for his closeup."

"You are kidding?" Francisco was totally surprised. "Oh, hell. Why not?" He laughed as they headed into the shop.

María saw them when they walked in. "¡Hola, Señor Andrew! You are back so soon. I thought you would not be back until next year. And with your friend, Señor Armando." Her face took on a strange look when she peered into Francisco's. "I do not understand.

How did your cut heal so quickly? There is not even a trace of it on your head."

Andrew grinned. "Huge change in plans. And just so you'll know, this is not Armando. It is his… nephew, Francisco."

"Really?! You could have fooled me. He looks exactly like Señor Armando. Handsome looks must run in the family." She placed her hand on her cheek in surprise. "Bienvenido, Señor Francisco. Any friend of Señor Andrew's is a friend of ours." She turned to a half-open door to the back. "Hector, come see who is here."

Shortly, Hector appeared. "Hola, Señor Andrew." He extended his hand and they shook. "Hola, Señor Armando." He extended his hand. He looked hard at Francisco. "How did your cut…"

María interrupted. "It is okay. Señor Andrew had a change in plans. And this is not Señor Armando."

Francisco took Hector's hand and shook it. "Hola. Francisco." He smiled.

Hector looked at Francisco then at Andrew and María. "But." Hector's face expressed extreme confusion.

Francisco, Andrew and María began to chuckle.

"This is Señor Armando's nephew, Francisco." María explained.

Hector shook his head. "Well, you could have fooled me. The resemblance is remarkable."

María smiled. "What can we do for you today?"

"I didn't know if you had the time but I was hoping Hector could take some pictures of Francisco."

Hector spoke up. "Certainly. I am not busy right now if that is all right with you."

"¡Perfecto!" Andrew called out and clapped his hands together.

As Hector got things ready to photograph Francisco, Andrew spoke with María. "I must tell you. Armando truly appreciated the pictures Hector took of him."

"I am glad. How is he doing? Where did he go?"

"He had to get to San Francisco. And he's doing… all right, I would say." Andrew looked up in the air then at María and smiled.

"Hector is right. It is unreal how much he looks like Señor Armando." She nodded her head. "And you know I want to hear the story you were going to tell me about Señor Armando. The one you said I will never believe."

Andrew chuckled. "One day, María. I'll tell you the WHOLE story about all this. And when it's done, we're all going to go have several cocktails because no one will believe it's true."

In less than an hour, the photo session was over and Andrew and Francisco were out the door. Next stop was the grocery store to stock up on a few things. The liquor store ended their trip and then it was home again.

—m—

Andrew made some Gin and Tonics and they headed to the beach. Francisco wore Armando's bathing suit since he didn't have one in his luggage from his trip to Europe.

"Thank you so much. I cannot wait to get the pictures back. I know they are going to be fantastic, knowing how the ones of Armando looked."

After a few hours on the beach, it was back to the house for dinner. As Andrew prepared it, Francisco went out and continued to look for more coins.

Just as Andrew was heading to call Francisco, he walked in with the bucket. "I found about fifty more. I think that is it. We can get a metal detector one of these days and check around the area to see if we missed any."

"I still can't believe how thoughtful Armando was to do that for me. He truly was a wonderful man." Andrew spoke softly.

Francisco placed the bucket in the closet with the other coins then went to the bathroom to wash up. They ate and went in to watch another movie.

Andrew made more Gin and Tonics, hot queso and a big bag of chips. "Okay. What's for tonight?"

"Pick one." Francisco smiled.

Andrew examined the collection of DVDs on the shelf. "Okay! Here we go! Something different but still a great classic. 'The Day the Earth Stood Still' with Michael Rennie and Patricia Neal. A wonderful science fiction."

"I have not seen that one, either. You seem to have a treasure trove of old movies I am not familiar with."

After the movie ended, Francisco sat back in his seat. "Now, that had an incredible message. And the music was great."

Andrew responded. "Mom and I used to sit up at night and watch the old movies on TV. There was a channel that played the old classic movies. She knew them from her mom. She said that on early TV they had the late show after the late news. They showed old movies from the forties and fifties. Of course, I fell in love with them. I've always wondered why they didn't make more like those nowadays. Guess everyone just wants to see things being blown up and action to the max. Oh, well. And I love the music in this movie by Bernard Herrmann. It's his music that set the music style for science fictions like that. He also did the music scores for a number of other great movies. Several I have here. 'Journey to the Center of the Earth', 'Psycho', 'North by Northwest', 'The Ghost and Mrs. Muir' and several more."

Francisco remarked. "'The Ghost and Mrs. Muir.' Is it a supernatural movie? I remember Armando referring to it in his journals and the letter to you."

"Well. Not in the sense you're thinking. It's a wonderful love story. Another tearjerker. Rex Harrison and Gene Tierney. A truly wonderful movie. All I have to do is hear the opening music score and I start crying." He shook his head. "Armando said he and Jacob will come for me like that when it's time." He stared off into space. "We can watch it one of these days, soon." Andrew picked up the two glasses, the empty bowl used for the queso and the empty chip bag off the coffee table and headed to the kitchen. "Guess it's time to hit the hay."

Francisco walked up behind Andrew as he stood rinsing out the glasses at the kitchen sink and whispered. "Andrew. May I be with you again tonight?"

Andrew turned and looked into Francisco's eyes and smiled.

CHAPTER XV

Andrew woke just as the sun was lighting the day. He couldn't believe the feelings he was beginning to have for Francisco. He remembered what he'd said in the very beginning that the only difference between him and Armando was their names. Could it be the same feelings Armando had for him were somehow carried into Francisco? Could he be so lucky to have another chance at love and not be alone?

He, too, began to evaluate what he was feeling. Were his feelings for Armando or for Francisco? He whispered. "'A rose by any other name would still smell as sweet.'" It seemed he was experiencing that expression for real. It was as if they'd been made from the same mold. They were virtually the same man. From what he could see, the only differences between Armando and Francisco were... their life experiences and their names. But if he did want to go further with Francisco, he had to know it was Francisco and not Armando. Maybe Armando was meant to pass through his life to pave the way for Francisco. Now, that's a thought. He began to move to get up.

"Stay with me." Francisco's voice was quiet. "Let me hold you a little longer. I like holding you."

Andrew moved closer to Francisco as Francisco's arm pulled him in. His head was next to Andrew's, his chin on Andrew's shoulder. He whispered. "Andrew, I... I..." He pulled Andrew tight against him.

Andrew felt overwhelming contentment. He didn't want to question anymore. He'd just let it unfold without prodding or poking. He dozed off.

When they awoke, Andrew didn't know the time but he didn't care. As he sat up, he turned and looked down at Francisco who was looking up at him, smiling. "Okay! 'Carpe diem!'" Andrew snickered. "I need to go fix us breakfast."

"I would rather 'carpe' you." He gave a big grin and winked his right eye. "But if we must get up, can I help? You are always doing for me. Please, let me do something. Something for you." Francisco pleaded.

"Okay. You can set the table. But I want to hit the shower first." He got up and headed to the bathroom.

"I will shower when you are done." Francisco called out. "But I could come in there with you. It would save on water." He began to chuckle.

"Yeah. Sure. Believe it." Andrew turned and started to laugh.

Andrew had the bacon in the pan and everything ready for an omelet when Francisco came into the kitchen. "Okay. Now, I'm not chasing you off but you've been here for several days. Isn't there someone looking for you or some secretary wondering your whereabouts?"

Francisco just called out. "Hey. When YOU are the boss, YOU get to call the shots."

"You know, you've never told me what the hell you have been doing. Yes. You did say you 'dabbled' but at what?"

"Whatever I want!" Francisco just smiled and began to giggle.

"No. Seriously. What have you been doing? In those twenty years since you found out about your uncle? Just curious."

Francisco looked right at Andrew. "You really want to know?"

"Well. Yeah. As long as you haven't been some notorious Axe Murderer."

They both just couldn't help themselves and broke into loud laughter.

"I will explain after we eat. I think we may want to sit down and kick back to go over it."

"Interesting. From the tone of your voice, it sounds like we'll need some Bloody Marys to go with that conversation." Andrew joked.

Francisco agreed. "That might not be a bad idea."

Breakfast over, Andrew poured the first glasses of Bloody Marys and they sat in the living room. To him, it was like a 'déjà vu', having done the same thing with Armando.

Francisco began. "How should I do this? You really should know it all but I do not want you to think I am a creep."

A questioning look came over Andrew's face. "Now, what could be so bad?"

Francisco looked down at the floor, at the two portraits on the wall and back at Andrew. "You know I was not going to say anything. That was the plan. I was going to give you the cross, the letter and then walk away. Regardless of the feelings, I had developed for you. I thought you would dismiss me after finding out all what Armando wanted you to know and go on with your life. But you did not. You were kind and good to me even in your grief. That only made me..." He stopped short and looked at the floor then took a sip of his drink.

"I guess the best place to start this would be to go back twenty years ago. Are you sure you want to hear it all?"

Andrew shook his head. "After that comment, what can I say? Now, I HAVE to know it all. And if we need more cocktails, there are more where these came from."

"Okay. You asked for it. You got it. And it is not a Toyota." A big Cheshire Cat grin filled his face. After a moment, he continued. "After my first visit to the Vargas law offices, that was the real eye-opener for me. No one in the family had any idea of all this. They thought the business journals were all there was. No one had taken the time to look into the Vargas firm. Of course, I was extremely interested in finding out more. Now, realizing I did have some minor family business obligations, I was traveling a lot afterward. But I would constantly be drawn back to finding out more about Uncle Armando. It was as if some unseen force was pulling me in that direction."

"I was constantly in their offices and reading Armando's personal journals. They were filled with incredible details of his month here with you. Not only did he explain the events that happened but he was very explicit in his writing down of his inner feelings about it all, too. Everything he described about you and what he felt for you and did with you. It was amazing. It was not a sordid story. It was a story of intense love and passion. And the entries he made were about his feelings over the years after returning to his own time. His love never swayed or altered. It actually grew more and more until the last of his entries before he died. His descriptions of you. I could not imagine such a man as you existing. So many I have met in my life have been deceitful, conniving and to put it bluntly, a bunch of liars. It is the reason I just had to know more about you and your life. Knowing who you were and where you were, made it easy. The one thing I knew I could not do was actually meet you. I could not disturb the timeline. I was afraid if I did, things could change and you may never have come to Zihuatanejo. You would never have saved Armando. And none of this would be as it is."

"Many years went by before I began to watch your career and life. The more I did, the more I came to care about and for you. Dare I tell you?" He looked up at the painting of Jacob and smiled. "In time, I even got to meet Jacob."

Andrew was so shocked he dropped his glass. He could hardly speak. "You met him? Jacob?" Tears began to fill his eyes.

"Oh, Andrew. I am sorry. I am sorry. I did not mean to upset you." He ran to the kitchen and got some paper towels to wipe up the mess. He poured Andrew another drink. "I am so sorry. I guess I should have prepared you for that before just blurting it out."

Andrew regained his composure. "Oh. No. It's all right. But you're kidding me? You met Jacob?" A little smile came to his face.

"Well. I actually got to know him."

"Really?" Andrew sat there dumbfounded.

"I knew all about Jacob from the journals and how you felt about him. I know this may sound crazy but in the beginning, it was for my research. Wanting to know all about you, only meant I would end up finding out about Jacob as well."

"How did you meet him?"

"I knew he was a fireman and a landscaper when he was not at the fire department. I also knew he was important to you. I knew he worked out of his house with the landscape stuff. Watching his movements, I realized he liked to periodically go to this little restaurant for lunch."

Andrew giggled. "I know the one. I told him he was keeping them in business as often as he used to eat there." Andrew shook his head and smiled in remembering.

"Andrew. I do not want to continue if this could be upsetting to you and hurting you."

"No. Please, go on. It's kind of nice helping me remember things. Keep going."

"Well. One day I watched him leave the house, knowing he was heading to the restaurant. I followed him. After he went in, I waited a little while then I went in. He had already ordered and was sitting alone, waiting for his food. I went up and made a small order and a drink. I got the drink and turned to see if I could get a seat nearby. But the place was so crowded, there was nothing close. That is when he saw me looking around for a place to sit. Realizing how crowded the restaurant was, he smiled, waved his hand and spoke, asking me to join him. I thought this was truly a stroke of luck. I could not believe I was actually going to meet him and talk."

"I have to tell you. I definitely understand what drew you to him. Yes, he was a very handsome man but his personality and graciousness outshined his good looks. We talked for several hours that day about his work and his interests. Finally, realizing the time, he said he had to go but if I was ever in the restaurant while he was there to please sit with him."

"I must tell you. We met there numerous times and I got to know more and more about him. I remember one day I walked into the restaurant and saw him. He just seemed to glow with happiness. He asked me to sit down and we talked more. I found out his birthday was coming up and he was turning thirty. I wished him a very happy birthday. That is when he told me there was going to be a party for him. It was going to be a 'surprise'. At least the person giving it, thought it was going to be. I can see him right now, smiling and chuckling."

"It was then he started telling me about..." Francisco stopped and looked directly at Andrew. "About you. Andrew, I could tell by his voice and expressions on his face how much he loved you. He expressed how kind and considerate you were to him and how wonderfully you treated him. One thing you may not have known. He told me you never thought yourself good-looking enough for him. You always thought he should be with some big handsome guy. He said you always thought about the kind of guys he should be with. Andrew, he thought you were as he put it, the 'cat's meow'. He said every time you were near him, he got so excited and turned on."

"You're kidding?" Andrew's mouth dropped open. "I know he always told me he was attracted to me when I asked but I always thought he was just being kind." Andrew shook his head. He was silent for a moment in a reverie. Then, he looked at Francisco. "I need a refill. How about you?" He got up, grabbed Francisco's glass and snickered. "I just knew he knew about the party but he acted surprised." He looked off into space reminiscing and a big smile filled his face. "I can see his face right now as he walked in the door." Andrew shook his head. "He put on a good show."

"Believe it or not, he wanted me to come to the party but I explained I had a previous engagement. That was not true but I knew I could not come to the party and meet you. I was living precariously by just talking with Jacob. I could be upsetting the timeline and I did not want to risk it any further than I had." He paused a moment and looked hard at Andrew. "You do not seem to be upset that I pried into your relationship and got to know Jacob. I think most would be angry at such an invasion. I did not mean anything by it."

"Not to worry. It's something I feel is so important with any relationship. I tell people there are three rocks in the road of all relationships. They are jealousy, possessiveness and the lack of communication. If both cannot get around them, the relationship is doomed. Neither one of us was jealous or possessive of the other and we always talked about everything." He paused for a moment. "You know. I do remember him telling me he'd met a guy in the restaurant several times, during lunch and how nice he was. He also said the guy was very good-looking. Just the type I liked." Andrew grinned and looked at Francisco. "I now know. He was talking about you. And you know what? He was right." A big smile filled his face as he paused slightly. "Francisco. I'm glad you knew him. It makes your connection and mine even greater."

Francisco continued. "But then there did come the time I knew I had to intervene, regardless of how it affected the timeline. It was in two thousand and five. I did not even think about it until the day was on top of me. I knew I could not say anything outright but I told Jacob he had to ask his May twelfth to thirteenth shift be altered, so he would not work that shift. I remember him asking why but I could not tell him. I was afraid he would dismiss it, so I made him promise. And he did promise he would."

"Of course, the night of the twelfth came and I sat in my hotel room, waiting for something to happen. I knew what I had done would obviously change the timeline. Uncle Armando would most likely die on that beach with no one to save him and I may never have been born. It was going to be catastrophic. I sat there waiting, waiting to just disappear, the instant the timeline changed. I knew I had probably killed myself but it was worth it. I knew I would be saving the life of a very fine and special man. And he was the one loved by someone I had come to know and care about. Strangely, the last lines of <u>A</u> <u>Tale</u> <u>of</u> <u>Two</u> <u>Cities</u> by Charles Dickens came to mind. 'It is a far, far better thing I do than I have ever done; it is a far, far better rest I go to than I have ever known.' At that moment, I knew how Sydney Carton felt. But I knew it was the right thing to do. And I waited."

"Finally, I saw the light of daybreak, coming through the window. I could not believe it. I was still there. Maybe the timeline had not been broken. I turned on the TV, knowing the early news would soon be coming on."

"There it was. Breaking news came on, regarding a major early morning fire in the county. I sat glued to the screen. Suddenly, there was an announcement. Someone had lost his life. I was shocked. Had the Fates corrected itself by taking the life of someone else? What had I done? They could not release the name until next of kin was notified. It was not until late morning when the news was updated that I found out. The reporter spoke. 'It was so unfortunate. A fireman who should have had his shift off was filling in for one of his comrades who had a serious family situation, needing attention. The fireman lost, most likely saved the life of the other fireman who is a husband and father of three children.' Then, the reporter said Jacob's name. It was almost earth-shaking to me. How could he forget? He had promised not to be there that shift. Did he not remember? But then, I understood. He was being himself, helping out a fellow fireman. Then, the news commentator spoke again. 'It is like something out of literature. Charles Dickens. <u>A</u> <u>Tale</u> <u>of</u> <u>Two</u> <u>Cities</u>.' Then, he spoke the same lines I had the night before. Andrew. I sat there and just wept for you. I knew your heart was broken into pieces and I could not go to you and help you."

Andrew's face was filled with tears and he began to sob. Memories of that morning came crashing back into his mind as if just happening. He bent his head down into his hands. "I remember. Jacob mentioned something to me about someone telling him to rearrange his schedule. And he did. But it was like him to help out someone else. That's why he went to work, filling in for another guy."

"Oh, Andrew. I am so sorry. I did not mean to bring all this up again for you and upset you. I just wanted you to understand. I think I am beginning to understand something myself. Sometimes, regardless of what we do, we cannot change things that are meant to be." He went over and pulled Andrew up and hugged him tightly.

When Andrew finally composed himself, they sat down again.

"Francisco, you were so incredibly unselfish to possibly and most probably lose not only your own life but your uncle's as well. And for someone else. What an amazing and unbelievably heroic thing to do."

"At the moment I heard it on the TV, I knew you had already heard. Yes, I began to weep, knowing your heart was breaking. I, too, had come to know Jacob and how kind and considerate and caring he was of others. And as I said, as much as I wanted to come and comfort you, I knew I could not. I had disturbed the timeline enough. I could not take any more chances with it. From then on, I would have to let things just fall as they were supposed to."

"I did continue to watch your life from afar. It would be less than a year before all the cards were to be played. I also knew I could not intervene and come here to save Armando. Things had to be as Destiny and the Fates intended. There was no telling the consequences if I tried to save Armando. The time had come and I was finally going to meet you in person. I knew right then it was I who was going to deliver the letter. No. HAD to deliver the letter and the cross to you. Andrew, you have no idea how happy that made me. I was finally getting to meet the man I had come to know and care about over the years from afar. The man I thought was cute and sexy the same way Jacob did. The man I had..." He looked right at Andrew. "The man I had fallen in love with. Andrew, I love you so much, I would gladly have given my life to save Jacob, knowing how much you loved him. It is the kind of love I had searched for in my own life. Giving up my life would have been a small price to pay." Francisco bent his head down.

"I so wanted to tell you the moment I saw you but I knew I had no right. I had no right to barge in on your emotions much less your life. And you had no idea who I was. I am sure you would have thought I was insane, making such announcements at that time." Tears began to run down his cheeks and into his beard. "Andrew. I love you. I love you more than life itself."

"Francisco." Andrew looked at him. "How could I not have feelings, strong feelings for you? You and Armando are truly the same man. I see that now. The only other difference is you don't have the same experiences Armando and I had. You've only read about them in Armando's journal. But it's okay. It's not experiences that make people care for one another. It's their personalities, their qualities, their hearts. I know now, caring for and loving Armando was the way to know you and open the door to caring and loving you." He smiled. "And I think of all the experiences we can share together if you're willing to take a chance with me. I believe I truly understand it now. It's like a revelation. I believe Armando was here out of his time, so I could get to know his person, his heart and to give him and share something he probably would never have found in his own time."

"But all those he knew and cared about would be lost if he stayed in this time. It might have been very difficult for him to remain in this time. He would've been the proverbial 'fish out of water' here. Yes, he'd have had a fortune with the jewels he had on him and would never have had any financial problems. But would that have been enough? Now, I know the one thing that was constantly on his mind. It was the knowing he was from another time and he might be pulled back at any moment. I now believe that could have weighed heavily on him and would have made a relationship very strained and difficult. In time, I'm afraid it might have been devastating to him. Maybe the Fates realized this, preventing his ability to ever cross back over the timeline again. He belonged in his own time. He knew how to deal with his life there."

He looked intensely at Francisco and smiled. "I also believe his journals were written, whether he knew it or not, for you." He paused for a moment. "And this land here. It was purchased and saved for this moment. Both of these things were to do just what they did. To somehow, lead you and me to one another. If not for his journals, I know you and I may never have met. This property was the place where it all could and had to happen. This is the place we would be drawn to. Francisco, you said it. You said the only difference between you and Armando was your names. You are so correct. One extremely important factor is you belong here. In this time. You know it and its history. And you are part of a family that recognizes your place in it. I swear the Fates work in such strange ways. It's one reason I tell people why I don't believe in coincidence. Things happen for a reason and we meet the people we do for a reason. We may never know the reasons but sometimes, all of a sudden, it just comes to us and is crystal clear."

Francisco smiled, nodding his head. "I cannot believe how overwhelming all this is and has been. Damn. I think I could use another refill." He held up his glass.

Andrew grabbed it on the way to the kitchen. "How about a walk on the beach? I think I could use some nice sea air right now."

"Sounds like a good idea to me. Bring a jug of your Bloody Marys, too. They are so good and they sure are helping me with the way I feel."

They had walked for a few hours just enjoying the day and the sea breeze. Soon, they leaned up against the rock that had become a favorite resting spot. Andrew opened the jug and filled their glasses.

Francisco spoke up. "Would you consider driving into Zihuatanejo and going to the boat shop I know of? I want to get a small sailboat and put it in the cove if you do not mind. I love sailing. Probably as much as Armando did."

"Certainly. But you have to promise me you'll never, ever, ever go out if there are any predictions of bad weather. I'm not losing YOU to the sea."

"Francisco gave a big smile. "It is a deal."

142

CHAPTER XVI

In time, Francisco's boat was delivered and placed in the cove. He would go sailing and periodically catch lobsters and fish for dinner.

In the meantime, Andrew started another painting. He couldn't resist, doing a portrait of Francisco which he hung on the other side of the one of Jacob. Francisco was completely overwhelmed by the gesture. Andrew told him, not only did the portrait belong on the wall where it hung but he belonged in the house as well.

He would call the business once in a while just to check on things. It seemed they were doing a great job of taking care of everything. He also called John, his taxman, asking him to file an extension as he'd not be back until June at the earliest. Andrew would also be asking John to give the name of a very good accountant who could organize all of his information needed for taxes in the future. Since he wouldn't be that involved in his business, an accountant would be needed to organize everything before sending it all to John for filing. He was happy to hear John's office staff could do that for him. He just had to have receipts and information submitted on a monthly basis by the catering company along with Andrew's deductions for his personal taxes. John also indicated his expected new trust fund would have to be carefully invested and taken care of. He suggested Andrew find a very good investment person.

Interestingly enough, Andrew knew a man in Atlanta who was an investment specialist. This man was nearing retirement age but just loved what he did. Many of the man's friends joked that with how successful he was, he'd probably never retire. Andrew's friend had spoken of him numerous times and knew he would be glad to help Andrew should he ever have money to do so. Yes. His name was James. James was extremely successful and lived with his partner, Albert, who was an engineer. They lived in the Buckhead area of Atlanta.

When Andrew contacted James and they finally met, he discovered that James' lifelong friend, David, had built a house not far from his own on the west coast of Mexico. David and his partner, Mason, lived full-time in Mexico but would come to Atlanta often.

Other friends of James were Richard and his partner, Roman. They lived in Atlanta but had built a retirement house not far down the beach from Andrew and Francisco. It was interesting to see Francisco and Roman together. You would think they were brothers, the resemblance was so uncanny. But their eye colors were different, Roman was a few years older and their life stories were significantly different.

All of these individuals would eventually become good friends with Andrew and Francisco.

Yes. Andrew was happy again. Francisco helped him through his grief for Armando and his constant reassurance made the bond they shared just grow stronger and stronger.

Francisco, too, was content. He had no worries since the family business was a well-greased machine. He had significant funds transferred to a bank in Atlanta and in Zihuatanejo. He also updated his credit cards, making Andrew's Atlanta mailing address his permanent one. He would now be living with Andrew. He hadn't been happier in his life. It was like everything he desired had fallen right into place.

Andrew placed photographs done by Hector and María as well as the ones he'd taken of Francisco and himself throughout the house to join the ones already there. He did the same at the Atlanta house. It was another way to let Francisco know he belonged there.

By mid-May, they'd gone back to see Manuel Vargas again with regards to the construction of the small chapel back on the hill. The recommended architect and builder were the same ones who built the original house. The design would be drawn up by late July or August with construction to begin in November. But with the upcoming holidays, it wouldn't be finished till after the beginning of the year. Due to the carved stone ornamentation that would be embellishing the structure, it could be late May before it was completed.

Francisco told Andrew this whole story just had to be told, it was so incredible. He thought it would make an interesting novel. He realized it would most likely become popular with only certain people but that didn't matter.

Andrew thought it would be fantastic. "Do you know I actually know a guy who is a writer? He just might like to write it for us. It should have a nice title, too."

Francisco scratched his beard with his right hand. "I've thought about it. All the events that occurred and you and me sitting here are the consequences of what happened in Zihuatanejo, starting over a hundred years ago with Uncle Armando when he first went to the Vargas Law Firm to buy this property and set it all up. That got the ball rolling. Then me, twenty years ago, going to the Vargas firm to investigate what I had found in the vault in Armando's house in Acapulco and discovering what I did. And finally, two years ago you coming to see Consuelo, the Vargas Law Firm and the boatbuilder in Zihuatanejo. Yep. We are here right now because of what happened in Zihuatanejo. So, I thought a good title would be It Happened in Zihuatanejo. What do you think of that?" He grinned and winked his right eye.

Andrew looked at Francisco and gave a big smile. "Wow. I like it. I think that would be a wonderful title. It Happened in Zihuatanejo. We'll go see him when we get to Atlanta again and tell him the whole story."

THE END

Printed in the United States
by Baker & Taylor Publisher Services